Twelve Days 'Til Trenton

TWELVE
DAYS
'TIL TRENTON

by John M. Duncan

Whittlesey House

McGraw-Hill Book Company, Inc.

New York   Toronto   London

Also by John M. Duncan
DOWN THE MAST ROAD

Library of Congress Catalog Card Number: 57-14688

Published by Whittlesey House
A division of the McGraw-Hill Book Company, Inc.
Printed in the United States of America

To the memory
of my mother and father
Agnes Taylor Duncan
William Duncan

1

MATT DOLIBER picked up his three-cornered hat from the ground beside him, settled it on his dark brown head, and rose with the others. He arranged his powder horn so that it would ride easily at his side, shifted the knapsack and blanket roll on his back, bent for his musket lying on the frozen ground, and as he straightened up, he looked into Tink Cooper's eyes.

"Tink," he said, "I've got to go forward and join my company."

Tink was half a head taller than Matt and much heavier, almost too heavy. "I don't know what you came down here for, anyway," he said.

"Gee, Tink," said Matt, "to be with you. Didn't we join the army together?"

Tink was sullen. "If you wanted to be with me so much you'd try to get into the company I'm in."

"I do try," answered Matt. "You know that. I've asked Sergeant Cummings for a transfer every night so far."

"Sergeant Cummings, Cummings, the caner," said Tink and there was a tinge of bitterness in his voice.

Matt was worried. "I've got to go," he said lamely and

7

turned away. Something was wrong with Tink. As long as he had known him, he had never seen Tink this way before. It was something deeper than the fact that they were in separate companies. It made him feel uneasy.

He moved up the road's edge to the First Company and looked for a place to break into the line. There was a spot open beside Adam Bean. He didn't want to take it, but he had little choice.

"Step in here, Matt," said Adam. "If you're like me, you'll be glad to get moving after three hours of preaching."

Matt didn't answer, but Jed Homan did. "I've heard longer sermons than that."

"Not in Pennsylvania," said Adam.

"We've only been in Pennsylvania three hours," Jed answered.

He was right. The Fourteenth Massachusetts Continental Regiment had been in Pennsylvania only three hours. As soon as they had crossed the Delaware River from New Jersey, Col. John Glover had called a halt and, with his foghorn voice, had delivered his Sunday sermon. The last time he had preached to his men was above White Plains in New York. That was a week ago. Since then the regiment had zigzagged across New Jersey, warily avoiding British and Hessian patrols, in an effort to join George Washington and the Continental Army.

Matt said, "Is it true that this is the last day we'll be on the move for a while?"

"Can't tell you that," answered Adam.

"Some of the men say this is the last day," said Matt.

Adam shook his head. "I've listened to so many stories

8

since I've been in this army, boy, that I ain't believin' anything till it happens, then I'm takin' that with a grain of salt. I gave up guessin' a year and a half ago when we first marched away from home."

Jethro Hatch joined the conversation. "And we been marching ever since. Do you know that for forty years, the furthest I ever walked at a stretch was from one end of a dory to the other, maybe twenty feet. I've sure made up for it since then."

"Jethro," said Adam, "when you joined the army you didn't walk, you rolled like you were still in a boat. Now you can get from here to there in a reasonable straight line."

"I sure get from here to there, anyways," Jethro said. "Wouldn't mind it so much if we stopped going backwards. I'd like to go forward just once."

Matt stared at Jethro. It seemed to him that the man was a little old to be in the army. He was the oldest man in the First Company. Matt himself was the youngest, not only in age, but in length of service. He had been a soldier for only a week. He knew, though, what the old man meant when he said he was tired of going backward. Ever since Bunker Hill, the regiment had fought and fled, fought and fled. He knew about Long Island and Pell's Point, Harlem, and White Plains, even if he hadn't been there. Now their retreat had taken them days away from Marblehead and the surf breaking over Peach Point and the scream of the gulls in Marblehead Harbor.

Sergeant Cummings came down the line. "We'll be shoving off in a few minutes, and we'll be moving pretty fast," he informed the men.

9

"We always move fast, don't we, Sergeant?" asked Adam.

"Sometimes we've had to," said the Sergeant, grimly. He spoke to Matt. "Well, Matthew, how do you like this war?"

Matt shrugged, but said nothing.

Sergeant Cummings smiled. "I've got a book I think you should read: *Militia Discipline* by a chap named Will Breton. It would help make you into a first-rate soldier."

Always something to read, thought Matt. Just because the Sergeant taught school back home, he didn't have to keep on giving out lessons. All that Matt could think of was Tink's nickname for him, "Cummings, the caner."

Shod hoofs ringing on the frozen road drew the Sergeant's attention. He saluted briskly as Colonel Glover, perched high on a solid gray horse, pulled up before him.

"The men shipshape?" barked the Colonel.

"Ready to go, sir," the Sergeant answered. "I've checked the company; the rest did them good."

"And the sermon, too, I hope," added the Colonel. Then he bellowed, "Hey, Jethro, Jethro Hatch! Patch up those shoes the first chance you get. I'd do it myself, if I had a bit of leather and an awl with me. You, Zeb Lacy, you look mighty peaked to me, you go see Doc Bond on sick call tonight. Boy," he spoke to Matt, "war's a lot of movin' about, ain't it?"

Matt looked up. "It seems so."

"Sir," added the Colonel.

"Sir," Matt answered and flushed.

"John," called Jed Homan, "will we be all done marchin' by tonight?"

"Can't say for certain, Jed. But there's one thing I do know, there'll be a shoal of generals around when we get where we're going, so don't you be calling me 'John' in front of them."

"I won't, John," answered Jed.

The Colonel wheeled the gray around before the men could see his smile, and cantered his horse back to the head of the line.

2

T HE REGIMENT moved off down the road in a column of twos and, for perhaps a mile, Adam Bean remained silent. Then he spoke without turning his head.

"You and Tink Cooper came from Marblehead together, didn't you?"

"Everybody knows that," snapped Matt.

Adam thought a minute. "I just can't picture Tink joinin' the army without a special reason. He ain't in trouble back home, is he?"

Matt was surprised. "Trouble! Why should Tink be in trouble?"

They were going up a short, easy slope. Adam waited till they reached the top, then he changed his line of questioning. "You left your Uncle Eb to do his lobstering alone?"

"Wasn't any lobstering to be done," said Matt. "Nor'-easter piled his traps on Marblehead Neck and made kindling out of them. Besides, the lobsters weren't crawling, it was too cold." His voice was becoming tart.

He should have known that if he gave Adam Bean a chance, Adam would ask him a lot of fool questions. It was his own fault stepping into line beside him. He had marched beside somebody else every day up till now. Just because Adam had been his father's friend, it didn't give the man the right to ask things that were none of his business.

They went up another slope, down a long hill, and pounded across a short bridge. Adam tried again. "What did Tink do, come up and say 'Let's go join the army' and you just picked up and came?" Adam watched Matt turn red.

"That's what I thought," he added. "Guess everybody in town knows that when Tink crooks his little finger you jump through a hoop."

Matt was too angry to reply.

Adam laughed. "Must have been a fine bit of business that scared Tink into the army."

"Nothing scared him in," flared Matt. "We talked about joining a lot of times."

"Yep," said Adam. "I bet Tink did talk about it a lot of times. Never did anything but talk. Never worked. Never went to school much. Beats me, with so many folks back home who are worthwhile, how you picked Tink for a friend. You ain't the kind of boy to take up with someone like him. Leastwise, you weren't when your dad was alive. You know, you ain't going nowhere 'sociating with Tink Cooper."

The regiment traveled on down the frozen road, sometimes in sight of the cold, flat Delaware River, sometimes away from it, past scattered farms and an occasional cluster of houses, with maybe a church or a general store lording it over the settlement. Mile after mile they marched, until midafternoon, when they fell out for a rest and a bite of the cold food in their knapsacks.

13

Matt avoided Adam Bean and sat down at the roadside between Jed Homan and Jethro Hatch. He looked down at Jethro's shoes, and quickly Jethro spoke.

"Heard Colonel John threaten to fix 'em, didn't ye? Well, I ain't fixin' 'em or askin' him to fix 'em. I'm waitin' till I'm lookin' down my gun sights at a Lobsterback or a Hessian that's got boots my size and I'm goin' to trade with him."

"Trade for those shoes?" asked Matt. "Nobody would trade for them."

"Yes, they would," said Jethro. He looked at his shabby boots. "I take his and give him mine, and throw in a little less pressure on my trigger finger for good measure." He gurgled. "Heh! heh! heh!"

Jed Homan laughed, too, but Matt didn't think it was funny.

Suddenly the clatter of hoofs pounding down the road brought them to their feet, muskets in hands.

"Shucks," said Jethro, "Philadelphia Light Horse. Seen 'em before. You'd think they were all rich by looking at those uniforms."

The riders dashed up to the head of the line and stopped. The leader, a captain, talked earnestly with Colonel Glover and his adjutant. Then with a salute and a wave of the hand, the horsemen wheeled and sped away down the road.

Adjutant Gibbs rode back to announce, "Two miles more to a place called McKonkey's Ferry, and we're there, Sergeant. Get your drummer and fifer up ahead. We'll give Mr. Washington and his army something to look at."

14

Sergeant Cummings called out, "Gardner! Pickett! Up front!"

Moses Gardner, swinging his drum into position and tightening the drumhead, moved up. Ben Pickett followed, fingering his fife to get the stiffness from cold knuckles. The musicians from the Second Company joined them.

Now the Fourteenth Massachusetts Continentals formed four abreast and filled the road from side to side. It was not a long line; there were barely two hundred of them, but in their neat double-breasted sea jackets trimly fastened with leather buttons, they were a fine sight. They waited smartly till the drums rolled, then they were off. It was easier going now, the drum cadence did that. They passed an outpost where the guards rose beside their fire and stared. They passed a few scattered buildings, but it was not until they reached McKonkey's Ferry and veered away from the river that the drums became full and the fifes quickened the blood in the men's veins as they shrilled "The World's Turned Upside Down." The tramping of the last week was forgotten. They were marching now, muskets aslant at the same precise angle, heads erect, chests out. Left, right; left, right. The shriek of the fifes, the beat of the drums, and the tramp, tramp of boots on the solid ground brought those who were already barracked along the road out of their flimsy tents, out of their lean-tos, from the barns and sheds where the luckier ones were quartered; and the men who had no shelter, but huddled about their camp fires, rose to watch.

General Washington, surrounded by a small group of

15

officers, was on the steps waiting as they halted before his headquarters in the Keith House.

So this was General Washington, thought Matt. This was the man for whom he was marching and for whom he would probably fight some day. He had often wondered what General Washington looked like. Now he knew. Tall, in his blue and buff uniform, taller by a head than any of his staff. Calm, very calm. Maybe just a little tired and a little sad, but strong. Strength seemed to flow from him. He watched the General warmly greet Colonel Glover, and he was sorry when they disappeared into the house. He wished the General had spoken.

At ease, the men rested, pleased with the effect their smart arrival had caused. "I guess that showed them," said Adam.

Three soldiers in buckskin hunting jackets leaned loosely on long rifles in front of the building. Two of the men wore fringed buckskin breeches, but the third, a boy about Matt's age, was naked from his beaded moccasin tops to his thighs. He wore a breechclout Indian fashion.

Adam Bean whispered, "Third Virginians. What a ruckus we had with them in Cambridge. If General Washington himself hadn't interfered we'd have driven them right back into Virginny. They do turn up a pretty good marksman, occasionally, though."

Before he had finished, one of the men drawled, "Wal, the Marbleheaders. Boys, what's the price of herring today? Ha! Ha!" He spoke to the breechclouted boy. "Brad, them's Marbleheaders from down in Massachusetts."

The boy shrugged. "I know they're Marbleheaders,"

he said. "Wasn't I in Cambridge when we had sort of a set-to with them? It's a good thing General Washington broke it up or we'd have driven 'em right into the ocean. Say, they do march pretty good, don't they?"

The tall man thought it over. "Even if they do wear them sailor jackets, they're pretty good soldiers, I guess. Ain't much on shootin' straight, but they did hold Howe and most of his army for a full day at Pell's Point. Didn't really lose either."

"Hey," he called. "You men got pretty good shoes. Is that because your Colonel was a cobbler once?" He guffawed at his remark. The other Virginian who had remained silent said, "They rowed us off Long Island. We sure would have catched it there, if they hadn't come along."

"Yep," said the tall man. "Somehow, they're almost always around, when we're goin' on a boat ride. Where's yore oars, Marbleheaders? You should carry them instead of rifles. Excuse me, I mean them blunderbusses yo're carrying."

Jethro Hatch could stand it no longer. "Anytime you feel like a rifle frolic, you let me know," he announced. "I'll shoot you for your pay, your vittles, or that Indian suit you're wearing."

"That's it, Jethro," said Jed Homan. "You could hold the frolic in a barn and you could try hitting one of the sides."

Everyone laughed but Jethro. Well, maybe he wasn't as good a shot as a lot of them, but Jed Homan, one of his own men, didn't have to bring that up.

3

A GUIDE from headquarters joined the Fourteenth and led them a mile up the road to a lane that ended in a plowed field along a frozen stream. "Knowles Creek," he announced and left them.

Matt didn't care about the name of the creek. All he cared about was the fact that he was going to share a flimsy tent with Adam Bean and Jethro Hatch on Sergeant Cummings' orders. He'd ask again, in the morning, to be transferred to the Second Company, so he could be with Tink Cooper. Sullenly he worked with the others to level a tent space for the worn sailcloth that Adam had gathered from the heap dropped by the baggage wagon.

"A good one," Adam said, as he dragged the canvas up and spread it out. "Not a hole or a rotted spot in it. Ain't a man in this company that shouldn't be as happy as a babe in this camp. I reckon it'll be almost comfortable. Of course, it ain't like sleeping indoors, but with a good fire to windward it won't be the same as sleeping outdoors, like a lot of them are doing."

"Ye'll be hard put to find enough wood for a good fire around here," said Jethro.

"That's the way it is in every camp, isn't it?" said Sergeant Cummings. "The first regiments to arrive get the most of it. I think there is enough for tonight, though. There'll be a wood detail in the morning."

It was almost dark when the cook summoned the men to the first warm food in a week. Turnips, and with the turnips he issued strips of beef that the men themselves skewered on the ends of bayonets and broiled in the coals.

"It's filling, if it ain't right delicate," said Jethro.

Matt wanted to get away from the men and join Tink, but before he had finished, the tall boy was standing beside him.

"Come with me," Tink said, abruptly. His dark eyes were half closed and his lower lip pouted in discontent. "I've got something private to talk about," he added.

Adam Bean, squatting at the fire, broiling his slim strip of beef, looked up but said nothing.

"Where can we go?" asked Matt.

Tink didn't answer, but started across the camp area. Matt left the warmth of the fire and tagged along behind until they reached the main road. There the boy turned and faced him.

"You sick of this?" Tink asked abruptly.

Sometimes Matt wasn't sure that he understood his friend. "Sick of what?"

"The army, that's what!" Tink's voice was brittle. "Sick of this marching and sleeping out and eating food that isn't fit to eat, and being cold all the time."

Matt thought before he answered. "I guess I kind of expected it when we left home," he said.

"Expected it!" snapped Tink. "Well, I didn't, and I'm getting out of here."

Matt was astounded. "You can't do that, Tink, that's deserting."

"What if it is?" answered Tink. "Dozens of men are deserting every day."

"Everyone was at roll call tonight," said Matt.

"Maybe everyone was here tonight," said Tink, "but they won't be here tomorrow night, because I'm leaving and you're leaving with me."

Matt's eyes widened. "Me! But Tink, you were the one who wanted to join the army."

"That was a couple of weeks ago. I had my reasons then. Things are different now. They're different for you, too, aren't they? How do you get treated? Cummings, the Sergeant—Cummings, the caner—the one who beat you half to death in school, now tells you every move you make."

Matt had forgotten about the cold. "He never beat me very much," he said.

"He would have if he could have found an excuse," growled Tink. Then he added, "If you want to know the truth, I made a mistake when I decided to join this army. I thought we'd be wintered in some warm barracks somewhere. How did I know there'd be nothing but marching and bad food, and cold and sleeping outdoors?"

"It's the same for everybody," said Matt.

Tink suddenly grasped the front of Matt's jacket in his thick fingers and pulled Matt toward him till their faces almost met. "Matt, me and you have been friends for a long time. We came here together. I spent all my money for us to eat and sleep getting here. Now we're leaving together. That's right, isn't it?"

Matt's mouth dropped open. He had never seen Tink this angry before. They had been friends for a long time, ever since Tink had come to Marblehead with his father who had opened a nautical instrument shop on Front Street.

"I guess I wouldn't want to go back to Marblehead," he said, weakly.

Tink's grasp relaxed. His voice seemed somehow filled with relief as he said, "I knew you wouldn't back out. I knew that." He clapped Matt's shoulder. "We won't go back to Marblehead. There's a dozen places where we can go and be better off than we'll ever be here. Tomorrow morning, first thing, come down to my tent, and we'll get out of here in a hurry."

It was becoming bitter, a bitterness that crept through their clothing and chilled their bones. Matt looked toward the camp. A dozen small campfires flickered, making shapeless lumps of the men huddled about them. He stomped his feet and blew on his fingers. "I guess I'd better go back," Matt said. Then he turned to Tink. "Tink, maybe I could get transferred to your company, then we wouldn't have to leave; we'd be together most of the time, on details and marches, and—" He didn't finish. Tink's face came down close to his again.

"We decided to go, didn't we?" Tink's voice was intense. "I'll see you in the morning." He turned and walked away leaving Matt standing in the cold.

4

IT WAS BARELY light when Matt heard
Sergeant Cummings' voice. "Adam,
Jethro, Matt. Do you want to sleep all day?" Matt was
up in a flash. Jethro snorted.

"Think we was farmers, the hour we got to get up!
Seems like I only been in bed about twenty minutes."

Adam yawned. "D'you think farmers get up any earlier
than fishermen?"

"Nup," said Jethro. "But I reckon it's a sight easier
to get up to go fishin' than it is to get up and go farmin'.
Mackerel, it's cold!"

From the next tent came the same disgruntled sounds.

"Guess we're all going for wood," said Adam.

Sergeant Cummings poked his head into the tent again.
"Get a move on, men," he ordered.

Matt was already out of the tent. Was it really morning? Tink would be waiting for him, he thought. He
fastened the big leather buttons on his short double-
breasted sea jacket, and set his hat firmly over his dark
tousled hair. He stretched and was as slim as an oar and
just as strong looking. It was cold out but the sky was
clear. Maybe the sun would come up soon and warm the
air a bit. He peered down the company street. It was

deserted. Tink should have told him in which tent he slept.

The Sergeant was checking the men: "Bean, Doliber, Hatch, Brimblecom, Homan, Lacy. The cook's got something for you and, when you've finished, draw rations to last all day. Maillet, the teamster, will be here before you're ready. He's almost harnessed up now."

Matt looked down the company street again. Where was Tink?

From the end of the First Company's tent row, a wagon appeared, the horses steaming in the dark morning air. How could he get away to meet Tink? Maybe he should say he didn't feel well, but if he did that, Cummings would have him on sick call in no time.

Adam spoke. "Real nice view, hey, Matt? Those tents all in a row sort of make me think of us when we're lined up for roll call. Better get something under your belt. We can't keep the wagon waiting."

Matt turned toward the fire to hide his flushed face.

Not until he had gulped his breakfast did he dare look down the line again. There was still no one about. What was he to do? It wasn't his fault he couldn't get away, with the Sergeant standing over him, and Adam watching his every move, and the wagon here and waiting.

The Sergeant spoke to the man on the wagon seat. "Got the axes, Maillet?"

"Put 'em in the wagon last night," answered the driver.

"Get your muskets, men, and climb aboard," ordered Cummings.

"Hey, Jethro," called Adam, "when you get your gun, bring out mine and Matt's."

23

Jethro grunted, but went into the tent and returned lugging the three muskets. "Looks like the oldest man in the company's got to do most of the work," he said. He handed Adam his gun and held out Matt's. When Matt was slow in reaching for it, Jethro shrilled, "Come on, boy, ain't you awake, yet?"

Matt sullenly took the weapon. He was as awake as he'd ever be.

"Climb aboard!" shouted Cummings. There was nothing left to do but to climb aboard. In spite of his anger, Matt had a feeling of something like relief once he was in the wagon.

"Where to?" asked the driver.

"Out to the main road," directed the Sergeant, "then turn toward the hills. There must be plenty of wood out that way."

Maillet, the driver, leaned over and cracked his horses with the ends of the reins, and Matt, like the rest, grabbed the bows that usually supported the canvas wagon top and did an involuntary jig as they jounced away in the frozen ruts.

As they swung onto the main road, they pulled over to let pass a wood-loaded cart driven by a tattered individual. The man had hardly any protection from the cold. The elbows of his light coat were gone, the fringed legs of his trousers were raveled far above the burlap bagging he had wound about his feet. His mittenless red hands holding the reins were raw. He pulled up alongside as Maillet called to him.

"Where'd you get that load?"

"In the woods, where'd you think?" The man was out of sorts.

"You must have been up plumb early," said Maillet.

"Got it last night and slept with it," said the man. "Just driving it in now. Say, I'll give you the whole load for a pair of shoes and one of those jackets you're wearing. Connecticut sent us down here and forgot about us. Now I don't care if the whole regiment freezes as long as I don't."

"Connecticut," shouted Jethro. "That's where they make wooden nutmegs and sell 'em for real, ain't it?"

"Sure is," said the driver. "Bring me back a good piece of hickory and I'll whittle you out a couple." He jerked on the reins, and as he pulled away he called back, "Keep on going till you get to the pickets. There's a lot of good wood out beyond them."

The sun had moved up above the horizon by the time they reached the pickets, but it was a weak sun and it wouldn't warm the air much today. One of the guards left the fire about which the group was huddled and reluctantly approached.

"Where's your pass?" he asked.

The Sergeant pulled out a piece of paper and handed it to him. The man looked it over halfheartedly.

"Wood detail." He shrugged. "Go into any wood lot you see that looks good. There's plenty of them a mile or two out. If anybody tries to keep you from chopping, tell him to go back home and write a letter to the Continental Congress about it. And don't forget to toss off a piece or two here, on your way back; we're running a little low." He strode back to the fire, blowing on his fingers and swinging his arms to get back the heat he had lost while he had been away from its warmth.

The wagon lurched on and as Matt bounced with the

rest of the men, he listened to their steady complaints about the cold, the early hour, the food, and everything that they could think of concerning army life.

If they detested it so much, why didn't they leave? Why didn't they all pack up and go home, he thought. Then suddenly he realized that the men were just talking. They really didn't mind it so much. He didn't mind it either. He had gotten up earlier than this many times to go lobstering. He had gone alone then. This was different. He was doing something with a lot of other people. It made him feel different, too. Sort of as though he were a part of something. He wished Tink would change his mind about leaving. Maybe he would by tonight.

"Maillet," shouted the Sergeant. "Pull up!" The wagon veered to the road's edge beside a thickly wooded lot and stopped, and the men scrambled to the ground, glad to be able to move about and warm themselves with work. Before Maillet had a brisk fire going, they had filled the wagon with wood found close by the road.

They worked and they rested beside the fire. Then they worked again, and Maillet shuttled between the men and camp half a dozen times, the men cutting their way deeper into the woods with each trip. It was late afternoon and they were gathered about the fire waiting for the wagon to return and pick up the last load, when a light brown flash bounded into the road just beyond them, paused, and with a tremendous leap disappeared into the brush.

"Deer!" shouted half the men almost together. "Deer!" Two men grabbed muskets and rushed to the spot where the animal was last seen.

"Come back," called the Sergeant. "It's gone." The men came back.

"Did any of you men ever hunt deer?" asked Cummings.

"I've never hunted," said Adam. "But my brother up near Danvers hunts, and he sends us venison every year. I've got a notion to go after that animal right now. Venison's real good eating."

"You'd run your legs into the ground trying to get it," said Jed Homan. "I've hunted. What we ought to do is get up a party and everybody go out together and try to round up a buck or a doe. If we got one we'd have some first-rate meat, for a meal or two anyway."

"That's what I was thinking," said the Sergeant. "Other regiments have details out looking for game most of the time. Would any of you men want to go?"

"Not me," said Jethro Hatch. "My shoes wouldn't stand it."

"What about you other men?" asked Cummings. "If Colonel Glover thought that there might be a chance of him getting a slice of venison, I think we could get a pass quickly enough."

Zeb Lacy spoke. "Never hunted deer in my life, but you can count me in."

"Me, too," announced Jed Homan. Adam Bean and Tom Brimblecom quickly agreed.

"What do we do?" asked Tom. "Net 'em, harpoon 'em, or use a hand line?"

Cummings laughed. "You know what to do, all right. Say, Matt, how about you? Don't you want to come along?"

It was Tom Brimblecom, whom Matt knew the least of

27

any of them, who spoke. "Better join us, boy. It might even be a bit of fun."

It was dark when they rode back to camp on the last load of wood, and when they arrived, Tink was standing in the shadows waiting for Matt.

Tink advanced on Matt and spoke in a voice so low that Matt could scarcely hear him. "Where you been?" There was almost a threat in each word.

Matt swallowed hard. "Getting firewood," he answered. "I looked for you this morning, Tink, honest I did."

"Come on," said Tink, and started for the road.

Matt hesitated. "I'm hungry," he said.

"Come on." Tink's voice was sharp. He walked away and Matt followed him.

When they reached the spot where they had talked the night before, Tink turned on Matt. "Are you leaving this place or not?"

Matt was slow in answering; there was no use making Tink angrier than he was now. He spoke carefully. "I was kind of hoping, Tink, that maybe you'd changed your mind today."

Tink almost exploded. "Me change my mind? Last night you said you were coming. Now you're trying to back out on a friend. Is that it?"

"I'm not backing out," said Matt, hastily. "But I had to go on a wood detail."

"If you had come down and got me this morning as you promised," Tink growled, "I wouldn't have had to stand guard over those boats hidden behind Malta Island. I nearly froze to death. If they think they can make me watch boats all day and then feed me turnips for supper, they're mistaken. I'm not going to do it. Matt, I'm giving you another chance. I'll take you with me in the morning."

"We'll never get away in the morning, Tink," said Matt. "There's always somebody watching."

Tink was silent for a minute thinking over Matt's words. He shrugged. "Maybe it would be better at night."

"That's right," agreed Matt, quickly. "That's when we've got to leave, when everyone is asleep."

Again Tink was slow in answering. Then he said, "That's a good idea, Matt. That's when we'll go, at night. We can get around the guards easy enough. I'll get some things together, food and an extra blanket or two."

"An extra blanket or two?" asked Matt.

Tink clapped Matt on the shoulder. "Don't you worry about that, Matty, my boy," he said lightly, "I'm just the one to get the things we need. It's all settled. Tomorrow night it is, and don't you forget it! I'm going back to the fire."

"I hope there's something left to eat," said Matt.

On the way back to camp he wondered where Tink could get extra blankets; then he forgot about it, as he tried to figure out why he would rather go hunting with the men in the morning than leave camp with his friend Tink.

5

MATT LAY FACE down behind a log at a spot where the sun played warmly on his back. He wasn't going to walk any farther. If a deer wanted to get shot, let it come and find him. He was tired but he was almost content. He would have been content if it were not for two people: Tink and Sergeant Cummings. Tink was a friend who seemed to have changed in the last week. Sergeant Cummings wasn't a friend. As long as he could remember, Sergeant Cummings had seemed to be against him. Way back, when he was in school and Cummings was the teacher, he was kept after hours more than any boy in the class. He remembered school too well. Extra work, always extra work— sums to do, verbs to conjugate, words to spell. Then, too, when he had rebelled at the work or when he was very wrong, there was the cane. Matt remembered the last time. It was long ago. His father was still alive then. "Matt," said the teacher, "this is a round hickory stick I have here, and I'm going to impress square root into you with it." And he did. Matt could still feel it, but no one could stump him on square root now. Even when the school term was over, Cummings used to bring books down to him. He had never looked at any of them. He had that book, *Militia Discipline,* right now, and he wasn't going to look at that either. Then he had gone to live with Uncle Eben, and met Tink, and hadn't gone to school so much any more.

Tink was something else again. He and Tink were going to leave that night. Tired as he was from hunting, he was going to leave. Why couldn't he go up to Tink and say he wasn't going? It was funny how many times he had asked himself that question during the last two days. He sniffed. He wouldn't think of Cummings or Tink or anyone. He rolled over on his back. He was almost warm. Wasn't it wonderful: the stillness of the woods. It was not like his sea, restless, surging, whispering and roaring, never completely at rest. He loved the sea, but this was wonderful, too, in its quietness, its feeling of peacefulness.

The sun caressed him through the leafless trees. The matting of fallen leaves beneath him was almost soft. He rolled over and cupped his hands behind his head, gazing at the blue above, cut into hundreds of angular shapes by the laced bare branches. There was a bird winging slowly across the sky. A seagull! It was like an old friend. What was it doing so far from the ocean? He wished he had the Portuguese spyglass. That would be something to look through. On the rare occasions when Tink had gone lobstering with him, he had brought the Portuguese spyglass from his father's shop. How Matt loved to use it. He could pick out boats in the harbor so far away you could scarcely see them with the naked eye. Once he watched a school of dolphin playing far off shore for half an hour; and the best of all was the time he saw the whale blowing off Catt Island. He took a deep breath, then yawned. He could go to sleep in an instant if he wanted to. Then he heard the faintest of sounds behind him. He hoped it wasn't one of the hunters from his company. He wouldn't want to be caught lying down. He rolled over and peered across the log on which his gun rested. He looked toward the sound for a long while. It came again, much closer; and from the woods into a little clearing ahead of him, daintily stepped a deer. Matt's heart suddenly pounded till he could hear it in his ears. The deer stopped, its head high, its nostrils flared. It knew something was wrong. Matt slowly rested the stock of his gun against his shoulder. He was trembling a little. The deer took a step forward. Matt looked down the sights of his musket and squeezed the trigger. The animal seemed as if on springs. It gave a leap that was never finished. In mid-air it crumpled and dropped in a heap.

Before Matt could rise, a figure stepped from behind a tree a dozen yards away. There was a smoking rifle in his hand. He grinned at Matt. "Seen you thar'," he said. "Too bad you missed."

It was a boy about the age of Matt. He was dressed in a buckskin hunting shirt and a breechclout. Matt knew him. He was the boy from the Third Virginia Regiment who was in front of headquarters when the Marblehead men had arrived. Matt was on his feet now. "Avast," he shouted. "That's my deer."

The boy's long, gliding stride had brought him to the dead animal. From his belt he pulled a hunting knife and slit the deer's throat, calmly wiped the blade on a fringed sleeve, and started to reload his rifle.

"That's my deer," Matt repeated. "I've been trailing him all day."

"Trailin' him flat on yore back," said the boy. "I've been watching you for 'most an hour. Better reload. You wouldn't want to be catched in these woods without bein' ready to blaze away, would you?"

The boy's advice irked Matt. He knew he should reload. "It's still my deer," he snapped.

The boy looked Matt over carefully. "I know you," he said. "Yo're one of them fish fellers from down toward Boston. Know them leather buttons anywhere. You men rowed us offen Long Island some time back." He shook his head at the thought. "That trip scared me more than Howe's whole army. Say, if you could only handle a gun like you handle them oars." He shook his head admiringly. "You know," he said, "I better get cleanin' that animal and start totin' it out of here."

"Don't touch that deer," said Matt. "I had a bead on him when I shot."

"Me too," said the boy calmly. "I aimed right behind the shoulder, and there's only one hole in him; look for yoreself. It's right behind the shoulder. If there were two holes I'd say let's clean him, and divide, but I don't see two holes, so I'd say this deer is rightly mine." He grinned cheerfully at Matt.

"It's not yours," snapped Matt. "That could be my shot. That's where I aimed."

The boy laughed. "I'm reasonable," he said. "I'm reasonable. If you can prove it's yores you can have it, but you can't prove it, and I think I can prove it's mine. In the fust place, who's most likely to hit what he's aimin' at?

Somebody who's been shootin' the eyes out of squirrels at fifty paces since he was four years old, or somebody who's been rowin' boats all his life? You want to know how I got in this here war? Well, I'll tell you. Word comes up to the Shenandoah country that Colonel Nabours is getting up a war party over in Winchester, so me and three hundred men from all over Virginia is mighty interested, and when we gets to Winchester, the Colonel says, 'Gosh a-mighty, I only want fifty men.' Then he thought a while and he says, 'I don't want to show no favorites so I'm puttin' up a target and everyone gets a fair chance.' So he takes a board and he draws a face on it with a piece of charcoal, then he marks a hundred and twenty paces and he says, 'That's King George the Third, his Royal Majesty, and anyone that can hit that head can go.'

"Do you know what I did? Well, I was first in line and I wasn't as tall as I am now. That was 'most two years ago, and the Colonel has to look down a little and he says to me, 'How old are you?' And I says, 'Almost fifteen.' And the Colonel says, 'Boy, yo're a mite young.' I says, 'Colonel, my name is Brad Ferguson and I walked here from Acorn Ridge yesterday. You said anybody who could hit that head could go. Don't you figure I should have a chance?' And the Colonel sort of scratches his head, and says, 'Acorn Ridge, that's a lot of walkin'.' And when he hesitates, I says, 'Can I have a chance, Colonel? I won't even try to hit him in the head. I'll hit him plumb on the nose.' 'Well, bless me,' says the Colonel. Then he shrugs and says, 'Listen, young man, if you can hit that nose at a hundred and twenty paces, I'll take you.' He turns and laughs to a couple of officers who are helping him. Boy, do you know

34

what I did? I just steps up and lets go and there's a hole right through the nose. Not only that, but the next fifty men who shot after me blew the nose right off. One of the officers says, 'Colonel, you wasted yore time drawin' a whole face,' and I figure he did, too." The Virginian had started to clean the carcass of the deer as he talked, using his hunting knife expertly.

"I don't see how that story proves this is your deer, and besides, you cleaning it doesn't mean it's yours, either," said Matt.

The boy straightened up. "Did you ever shoot a deer before?" he asked.

Matt shook his head. "No, but. . . ."

The boy interrupted him. "Then you had buck fever," he said calmly. "Nothin' to be ashamed of. Lots of people get buck fever. They can shoot anything till they level down on a deer. Can't explain it, myself. No matter how big the deer is, or how close it is, they miss. That's what you had, a touch of buck fever. Some people never get over it. You know up till now, I been tryin' to convince you by talkin' and I was kind of hopin' you'd be reasonable. Now I got to prove this buck is mine for sure. Yo're shootin' a musket, am I right?" He pointed the knife blade at Matt's gun. "A smooth bore?" the boy persisted. Matt nodded. "And an ounce ball and about two ounces of powder?"

"Everybody does," said Matt.

"Everybody that spends their lives rowin' boats around," agreed the boy. "Me, I'm using a rifle with a half-ounce ball and an ounce of powder. Now, when you shoot and hit anything with a musket, it either smashes it

35

to bits or puts a hole in it you could put yore fist into. That's 'cause the ball don't spin none in the air. With a rifle, the ball is spinnin' like a top and it makes a real clean hole because it bores in. Look"—he pointed his dripping knife to the wound—"clean as a whistle! Now look at that birch tree. 'Tain't even in the line of fire."

The birch was ten yards beyond the carcass of the deer and there was a fresh shredded tear that went completely through it head-high and about two inches in from the edge.

"A bullet to have made a hit like that would have to go over the top of the deer's shoulder. That's a real buck-fever shot," the boy continued, "high and a little wide. Nothin' to be ashamed of, like I said; a lot of good men get buck fever."

Matt was aghast. "That could be your shot," he blurted.

The boy stood up, wiped his hands, and grinned again. His face was fresh and brown and a ridge of freckles crossed the bridge of his nose and scattered beneath his good-humored gray eyes. There was something about him that wouldn't let you become real angry with him.

For the first time something inside Matt told him that the boy was right. He watched as the Virginian laid his knife on the deer's flank, rose, picked up his gun, and walked back a score of paces. "This is about the right distance," he said. Yo're a hard man to convince, but this might do it." He turned, aimed the gun at the birch tree, and fired. On a line with the first hole torn in the tree and exactly the same distance in from the opposite edge was a clean round hole that might have been bored by an auger.

As the boy returned, his eyes held a sympathetic gleam.

"I'm Brad Ferguson, like I said," he announced. "You know, there's 'bout three hundred men back in camp, all from Virginia, and a buck like this won't go too far, but if you'll give me a hand at gettin' it back there, I wouldn't be agin lettin' you have a quarter, maybe."

The boy wiped his hand on the tail of his breechclout, and held it out.

Matt hesitated, looked down at the ground, and worried a dead leaf with his toe. Finally he looked into the boy's gray eyes, and took the hand. "I'm Matt Doliber," he said. "And I guess I did have buck fever. How are you planning to get it back?"

"Tote it," said Brad. "It's been eatin' a lot better than we have, but it can't be over two hundredweight, cleaned." He reloaded his rifle as he spoke. "Can't drag it. Ain't enough snow cover. It would cut the hide to pieces, and that hide is a new pair of leggin's for me—my legs get quite cold this time of year—and mebbe a couple of pairs of moccasins. Might even give you a pair of moccasins. Don't know how anybody can walk in hard boots."

"Must be five or six miles back to camp," said Matt.

"Must be," agreed Brad. He was working on the deer again. Finally he stood up and said, "Clean as a whistle," wiped his hands, and handed Matt his knife. "Why don't you start whittling on the beech tree up there on the rise? We need a pole about that size." He pointed to a slim beech still hanging onto its long-withered fawn-colored leaves. "That one will be about right. I'll be up as soon as I tie this critter's feet. We'll shove the pole through 'em, and we shouldn't have any trouble getting the deer back." Matt looked over the animal again. It looked like a tremendous load to him, especially for just a quarter share.

Brad pulled a piece of rawhide from somewhere and Matt made his way to the top of the rise. From there he looked, and looked again. Quickly he turned. "Hey," he called. "A house and the river."

Brad stopped trussing the deer's legs and rushed up to join him. Trees extended down the slope for a distance, but through them could be seen a fence surrounding a large field, on the far edge of which was a house and barn. Just beyond the house was the road. Alongside the road was the river.

"Criminey," said Brad. "The road. When we get on it, we got easy totin' all the way."

"Totin', nothin'," Matt said, mimicking the boy. "I'm going back to Malta Island and get a boat. We can leave the deer at the farm. Rowing it back won't be anything, at all, and we won't need a pole to get it down to the river. We can carry it that far."

6

MATT LAY in the woods just short of the fence, panting and warm. Brad rested beside him. Between them was the deer, which Matt had carried over the slope and down almost to the fence. He had never struggled under a heavier load. Even the two of them could never have carried the dead weight six miles back to camp.

"Better stay here awhile and watch that place," said Brad. He nodded his head toward the farmhouse. "Maybe a company of Hessians are taking tea there, right now."

"Not on this side of the river," said Matt. His voice still came in little gasps.

"We'll watch anyways," Brad continued. "Then if we don't get any hostile signs, we'll go up and maybe we can borrow a wagon and get this deer down to camp."

"Wagon," said Matt. "What's wrong with a boat? I can get to Malta Island and pick one up in no time at all. You could wait at the house till I got back. Maybe they'd let you wait inside where it's warm."

"What's wrong with a wagon?" asked Brad, sharply.

"What's wrong with a boat?" Matt's voice was just as sharp.

Neither boy answered the other's question. They sat

silently watching the house. Once smoke came from the chimney, and Brad said, "Someone's there, anyways."

"Stirring up the fire," answered Matt.

They waited awhile longer for other signs, but saw none. "Come on," suggested Brad, "let's leave the deer here and go up and see if they have a wagon."

Matt said nothing. They rose, picked up their guns, and slowly approached the fence. The house was not very far away. They watched it for a short time and then slid their guns under the fence and were about to scramble over it, when a door swung open and a figure in a swirling dress came flying out. The figure carried a gun with both hands and advanced swiftly as if it were a bayonet charge.

"Don't you dare touch that fence! Don't you dare!" she shouted as she bore down on them.

The boys looked at their flying assailant, until she came to a stop a dozen yards away. There she planted herself, feet firmly apart, and raised the gun to her shoulder. "Don't you touch those rails," she warned. The muzzle of the gun wobbled every which way.

"It's a girl," said Matt and Brad together.

It was a girl with light yellow hair in two heavy braids.

"We don't want yore fence," said Brad hastily, "and you better put down that gun 'fore it goes off and kicks you all the way back to the house."

"You can't have those rails," persisted the girl. "I know that's what you want. You'll take them down river and use them to build something, I know. We're the only people around here with a fence left."

"We don't want your fence," insisted Brad. "And now

that I've seen yore gun closer you can put that down, because you ain't goin' to hurt anyone with it."

The girl looked a little uncertain. "Why, you're just boys," she said.

Brad grinned. "Miss, I'd just as soon you shot me as said that."

The girl almost laughed. She did lower her gun.

A blob of a man carrying a pitchfork came waddling up and stopped beside her—a man not much taller than the girl and almost as wide as he was tall. "Paula, vot iss?" he panted.

"Papa, they are just boys," she said.

"Shust boys? Shust boys? They iss soldiers. Vot iss it they vant? The fence?"

"We don't want the fence," said Brad. "We got a deer over in the woods. We want to take it back to camp."

"A deer?" The man did not understand.

"That's right, mister," said Brad, "a deer."

"Vy you come this vay?" the man asked, suspiciously.

"We got him just over the hill, and we thought maybe we could borrow a wagon."

"Papa," said the girl. "That was the shooting we heard. They shot a deer."

"They don't vant no fence or nothings?" The man's voice sounded relieved.

"That's right, mister. All we want to do is borrow a horse. . . ."

"Ve got no vagon, ve got no horse. Mels, my boy, he's in the army with the horse, till spring. You know him? He's mitt General Muhlenburg. Otto und Willem are in the var, too."

41

The tension was gone. Both Matt and Brad breathed easier. Matt spoke for the first time. "We'd just like to leave the deer here till we get a boat. That's all, mister."

The man stared at Matt. Then he pointed a chubby finger at Brad, and spoke excitedly. "Him, I don't know ver he iss from. But him"—his finger swung over to Matt—"him I know from ver he iss. Massachudsetts. Look, Paula, look, dot sea jacket, und dot agcent. Massachudsetts. He's a blue-water sailor. Dot I know. Ver from, boy? Glowster? Salem?"

"Marblehead," said Matt, amazed at the question.

"Mobblehedt! Mobblehedt! Paula, Mobblehedt! You hear? Scoot back by der house und put on the kettle. Mobblehedt! Thirty years ago I fish oudt from Glowster; lots of times I been by Mobblehedt. Boys, you bring the deer. I vill let you haf a boat. One of them I haf. You go get that deer. Me, I'll be by the house ven you come." He turned to waddle after the girl.

"We got a boat, didn't we?" said Matt, elatedly, as they went back to the woods.

Brad was not very enthusiastic. "Say, did you see that girl? You know what we do with girls like that out back of Winchester? We drown 'em when they're three weeks old."

"She's a Tartar," said Matt. "I hope I don't have much more to do with her. It's your turn to carry the deer."

42

7

THE SHORT, fat man met them at the door. There was wonder in his voice. "Mobblehedt," he said. "For thirty years I don't see anybody from Mobblehedt."

Brad stood under the weight of the deer. An old dog lazily moved up to sniff at the carcass.

"Take it in the barn," directed the man. "Shut tight the door so Fritz don't get it." He nodded toward the dog. "You"—he pointed at Matt—"you come in. Tea ve got, und bread und jam. It don't take two."

Matt looked uncertainly at the Virginian. Brad looked as if the weight of the deer would crush him to earth any moment. He shifted it on his shoulders. "Go on in," he said. "It don't take two." He lurched away toward the barn. Fritz trailed after him.

Matt kicked his feet clean on the edge of the stoop and followed the man into the kitchen. The girl who had threatened them in the field was busy with a kettle and teapot. She looked up at Matt as he entered, but she said nothing. Her pretty red mouth was set in a prim line, but her clear blue eyes had little crinkles at the corners. With her round, smooth cheeks, she was pretty. Matt didn't speak.

The heavy man pulled out a chair at the table and said,

43

"Sit. Me, I'm Klaus Kinderhook." Then he turned and beamed at the girl. "Und this iss Paula," he added, "who now takes care of her old papa und her brothers ven home they are."

The girl paid no attention to the introduction, but kept busy, selecting dishes from the cupboard.

What a cupboard, thought Matt, all covered with odd-looking flowery designs in all sorts of colors; everything had designs on it, the chest, the chairs, the cupboard.

"Her mama came from Lancaster," said the man, following Matt's eyes. "Me, I shipped from Glowster to Philadelphia und I never go back, I never go to sea again, either." He shook his head. "Now, Mama iss gone."

He sighed deeply, then quickly he spoke again. "Paula, the bread und jam. So long you take." Then he turned to Matt and talked away while the girl brought crockery, tea, a tremendous loaf of white bread, and a pot of jam. As she put the last of it down, she addressed her father.

"He didn't tell us who he is, Papa," she said.

Matt flushed as the girl turned toward him and looked him full in the eyes. How blue her eyes were. He said, "Matt."

"Matt?" The girl spoke to him now.

His tongue seemed tangled. "It's sort of short for Matthew," he managed to say.

The girl looked at him coolly. "Is that all?" She handed him a piece of bread covered with strawberry jam.

This girl was trying to confuse him. "Matt Doliber." His voice was almost a mumble and he could have kicked himself.

"Paula," her father warned, "don't you go fussing this

44

boy. You talk to the other one ven he comes in. I talk about Mobblehedt, to him." He pointed across the table.

"Thirty-fife years ago it vas. The brig *Katrina* foundered off Norman's Woe. You know Norman's Woe? Me, I vas picked up und took to Glowster where I stay und fish."

There was a knock at the door and a scuffing of feet. It was Brad.

As Paula crossed the room, Matt wondered if she always carried her nose that high.

"Come in," she said brightly as she opened the door. Brad grinned.

"Yes, ma'am; it's sure been a spell since I've been inside a house, and warm, too."

"Boy, vot's your name?" said Mr. Kinderhook.

"Brad Ferguson. I'm from Virginia."

The girl cut in. "I guess you were scared I was going to shoot you, weren't you? And I would have too, if you had touched a single rail of that fence."

"Guess I was at first," answered Brad. "But then when I looked things over I wasn't worried a bit, seein' as the gun wasn't loaded."

"Wasn't loaded?" The girl's eyes grew big.

"That's right, ma'am." He nodded toward the gun standing in the corner. "Just look it over kind of careful like. I think you'll find that there's a snapper where the flint should be, and a snapper ain't goin' to make a spark. Come here, I'll show you."

Brad walked over and picked up the gun. In the jaw that held the flint was a small wooden peg. "Someone put that in there to keep from wearing out the flint when the

45

trigger was pulled and the gun wasn't loaded. Next time you want to protect that fence for sure, you better pull that snapper, put a flint in, and load up. A gun ain't too effective from a distance this way."

Brad grinned again, and the girl grinned too.

"I scared you for a minute, though," she said.

Matt wondered why he couldn't talk like that to a girl and not have the few words he could muster come tumbling out mixed up.

"Paula," thundered her father, "don't stand by the middle of the kitchen all day. Give the boy somethings to eat. Take him over by the fire. So he can get varm. Mittoudt pants, cold he must be."

" 'Tain't so cold when you get used to it," said Brad.

"Here," said Mr. Kinderhook. He shoved a cup toward the girl. "Mitt tea fill it, und get some bread und jam, und leave me und him." He nodded toward Matt. "Ve talk about Massachudsetts."

Brad walked over to a long bench beside the fire; and Paula filled the cup with steaming tea, put a generous layer of jam on a fat slice of bread, took it to Brad, and sat down beside him.

Papa was asking all sorts of questions about boats and fish and Gloucester and Marblehead and Salem and the people he remembered who lived there.

Matt ate more and had more tea and answered the man's questions, when he knew the answers, without thinking too much about them. With one ear he listened to Brad and the girl near the stove. They chattered and laughed as if they had known each other for years. Once when she was laughing, he looked in her direction, and his face grew

46

red because she was looking at him. He turned quickly back to Papa.

"How far is it to McKonkey's Ferry?" he asked.

"By the river, four miles," said Klaus Kinderhook. "By the road it iss longer. I let you take a boat to get the deer down. It's not my boat, it's Mels' boat. Mels iss my boy. He hunts duck from dot boat. You vill bring it back?"

"I'll bring it back the first chance I get," promised Matt.

"A big boat it iss not," explained the man. "But for you und the deer und him," he pointed to Brad, "it iss big enough. Paula."

The girl looked up. "Yes, Papa."

"Ve don't have venison since Mels vent in the army."

"No, Papa," answered the girl.

The man turned to Matt. "Willem und Otto vork on the farm, but Mels"—he raised his hands high—"hunt und fish all the time." He shook his head sadly. "Venison, ve don't have since Mels goes mitt General Muhlenburg."

The girl stood up suddenly. "Papa," she said, "ain't you ashamed talking like that about venison? Besides, it's getting dark and the milking isn't done."

"Ach," said Mr. Kinderhook, and pulled himself up from the table. "You," he nodded at Matt, "you vill come back?"

"I'll bring the boat back," said Matt.

"Und ve vill talk some more. Thirty years I don't see someone from near Glowster." He waddled to the door. "Paula, you know ver iss the boat."

"Yes, Papa," said the girl. Brad rose. Paula came only to his shoulder. "I'll show you the boat," she said. "The oars are under it." She threw a shawl over her shoulders.

Mr. Kinderhook turned at the door. "You boys, both come back und Paula a snitz pie vill make."

"Papa," said Paula, "we don't have any yellow apples for a snitz pie."

"Ve make it from the red ones, then. In the cellar they are." He almost blocked up the entire doorway going through it.

Matt and Brad followed Paula into the open. She led them through a gate and across the road where a path led into a thatch of willows by the river. Here, high on the bank and chained to a stump, was a small boat upside down. "The oars are beneath it," said Paula, "and there is an old dipper, without a handle, for bailing."

"Eight foot anyways," said Matt, "big enough. Why don't you go back for the deer?" he spoke to Brad. "And I'll get this into the water."

Brad looked skeptically at the boat. "You mean you and me and the deer can all go down the river in that?"

"That boat would carry a lot more than us," said Matt.

"But I heard Paula's father say it leaks," stated Brad.

Matt shrugged. "From the looks of it, it doesn't leak much. You can bail if it gets too bad." He unwound the chain from the stump.

"Maybe we better go back to camp and try to get a wagon," persisted Brad.

"Maybe we better get the deer. It's almost dark," said Matt.

"I'll get it," said Brad. He turned quickly back toward the barn.

48

Matt expected Paula would follow Brad, but she stayed beside him. "I used to help Mels put the boat in the water," she said, and when Matt bent to tip the boat right side up, she lent a hand. Beneath it lay the oars, old and with most of the paint gone, but solid looking.

"Now we pull it down," said Paula. With one of them on each side, it slid down the bank and into the water easily. There was only one place where the water seeped through—a crack in the planking less than a foot from the bow.

Matt handed the chain to Paula while he scrambled up the bank for the oars. When he slid back, he said, "With the deer and him," he jerked his head toward the barn, "in the stern, the bow will be high enough out of the water to stop that leak." He threw the handleless dipper into the boat and took the chain from the girl. They said nothing for a minute, then Paula spoke.

"Are you coming back?"

Matt shrugged. What did she mean by a question like that? She had heard him say he would bring the boat back. He reminded her of that.

"I've got to bring the boat back, haven't I?"

"If you didn't have the boat would you come back?"

Matt didn't know what to say. He let the boat catch itself in the current; and when it swung away from the shore he pulled it back with the chain. When he looked at Paula, her nose was as high in the air as it had been in the kitchen. "I was thinking of Papa," she said. "I haf not heard from him such talking. . . ." She stopped and stamped her foot. "I have not heard him talk so much since Mels went away."

49

Matt let the boat float out into the current again. He'd patch that leak before he brought it back up river.

"Hey!" It was Brad standing above them bent beneath the deer. "Help me get this down."

Matt handed the chain to Paula and together he and Brad lowered the deer. Paula swung the boat so that Matt could step into it. He helped load the deer until it lay stiffly across the gunwales near the stern. "Hand me the guns and the oars and hop in," he said to Brad.

Brad picked up the oars and handed them to Matt. He then handed Matt his musket, but hung onto his rifle. Matt laid his gun in the bow, slipped the oars into the oarlocks, and sat down waiting for Brad to step aboard. Brad looked at the trickle of water from the bow. "It leaks," he said.

"When you get in, there won't be any water coming in," Matt assured him. "Your weight will raise the bow out of the water so high you could walk under it."

Paula spoke. "It's almost dark, I'd better go," she said. She dropped the chain in the boat and ran up the bank and across the road without looking back. Matt watched her till she disappeared, but Brad didn't take his eyes from the boat.

8

BRAD FERGUSON had his doubts about the safety of the boat. He hesitated till Matt had to urge him on.

"It's dark," Matt said. "We'd better get started."

Brad stepped gingerly into the stern. It was a tight squeeze between him and the deer. Matt at the oars was almost as crowded.

The Virginian sat himself squarely in the center of the seat, a hand on each gunwale as if to balance himself, his head stiffly set at dead center. The boat swung into the current by itself and Matt guided it downstream. Then Brad's eyes found the water, and he seemed fascinated by it. "Couldn't we sink?" he said; his voice was filled with misgiving.

Matt looked along the side. "Sink?" He laughed. "We're deep because we've got a heavy load. There's a good two inches clear. Say, if we go under I'll toss you an oar. You can float forever with an oar. Old Seth Bemis tipped over in Lady's Cove a couple of years ago, when he was rowing back from the cider mill. He grabbed the two jugs he had, put one under each arm, and put his chin over an oar. Half an hour later someone saw him and rowed out and picked him up. Those jugs were filled, too." Matt did not know whether Brad responded or not to the story. He was too amazed at the amount of talking he had been doing.

He heard Brad say, weakly, "I can't swim a lick."

"I just told you, you don't have to swim if you've got something that floats and you know how to use it." Matt peered at Brad in the dark.

Brad was as rigid as his rifle, each hand still gripping a gunwale as though it were frozen there. Then Matt realized that Brad was actually frightened. He couldn't conceive of a man in a sound boat, well, almost a sound one, on a smooth stretch of river, being frightened. He finally spoke. "You're scared, aren't you?"

Brad answered, honestly and emphatically. "I guess I am. I ain't scared of nothin' but water. I ain't scared of rattlers; I ain't scared of Injuns; I ain't scared of war; but I'm awful scared in a boat. I pretty near died gettin' onto Long Island and off it, and I ain't never goin' near that Hudson River again till they build a bridge."

Matt stopped rowing and leaned on his oars. "The road here runs along the river. Why don't I let you off and you can walk back? I'll meet you behind Malta Island. That is where all the boats are anchored. You ought to get there as soon as I do."

Brad hesitated before answering; then he said, "I wouldn't want it to get around...." His voice trailed off.

"I tell you what," said Matt, "if the fact that I missed that deer doesn't get around, I guess the fact that you're just a little nervous on the water won't."

"Sailor," said Brad, relieved, "I guess I'm plumb agreeable to that, and I figure that I'll give you half the deer in the bargain."

Matt swung close to the bank, spun, and backed in stern first. Brad, rifle in hand, was ashore as the boat ground into the bank. He didn't speak a word, gliding into the darkness as though he had cat's eyes.

It was bitter cold and it was black, but Matt had a boat under him. Now, he'd really row. His arms stretched out and the blades of the oars cut silently into the water. With long, strong pulls he shot the boat ahead. The oars left long spaced eddies in the water and trailed strings of droplets to the next eddy. In the dark it felt as if he were skimming over the surface, barely touching the water. He felt his own strength on the oars. Maybe he did get buck fever, but he didn't get water fever. This was what he knew and loved. It made his blood sing in his veins. For a long time he pulled away, and then he rested. Warm and breathing hard from the exertion, he leaned on the oars and let the current carry him. Then he rowed again and rested again. It had been a long time since he had felt so good about everything. Then he remembered Tink. This was the night they were going to leave camp. The thought should have upset him, but it didn't. He'd explain to Tink, when he saw him, why he wasn't able to leave. It would have to be some other time. Not tonight.

He rowed again for a long time and when he turned to check his bearings there was a faint glow against the low-hung clouds. Campfires, he thought. He turned in toward shore and rowed down at slower speed. He kept on till a voice shouted, "Halt, who goes there?"

"Matt Doliber," he shouted back. "Fourteenth Massachusetts."

53

The voice rang out again. "Advance slowly and give the password."

The waves from Matt's boat lapped against a fleet of others lined up against the shore. He could see figures before a low fire.

"Charity," called Matt, loud enough to be heard.

"Matt Doliber, you mackerel hound, 'Charity' was the password last night." Matt grinned to himself in the dark. It was old Jethro Hatch.

Jethro's voice sounded again. "There's a half-Indian without pants up here, and he says you got a deer aboard. I ain't believin' it till I see it, so pull ashore."

9

I T WAS HARD for Matt to realize that it was already morning when Sergeant Cummings shook him. "Roll out, Matt," he said. "Adam, get moving."

Adam Bean sat up, stretched, and leaned over and shook Matt again. "You awake, Matt?"

Matt could hardly get his eyes open. "What's the matter?" he asked.

"We're goin' to Trenton," said Adam. "Cummings and me got orders last night, and we figured it's about time you learned there's more to soldiering than marching and hunting deer. You know, everybody in camp is talking about you getting one."

Matt pulled himself to his feet. "Just got half a one," he said, yawning.

"That's a half more than anyone else got."

"I haven't got it yet." Matt stuck his head out of the tent and pulled it back quickly. "Brr," he said. "Isn't it ever going to get warm? I don't get it till Brad skins it and divides it."

Jethro Hatch rolled over and lifted his head. "If you men want to hold a conference, why don't you go out and find a meetinghouse?"

"This'll make you happy," said Adam. He threw his

blanket over the old soldier. "Let him use your blanket, too," he said to Matt. "You won't need it today."

Sergeant Cummings spoke to Matt as they huddled about the low fire and drank hot tea. "This is your first scouting trip, Matt. Just do the same as Adam and I do. It's a good chance for you to learn a few things. I've got a boat picked out. Adam will row. We'll take it halfway down to Trenton and hide it, then go ashore and see what we can see. Pack a day's rations and no more. Now, you'd better check everything, powder, lead, water."

Matt wondered if there would be any fighting. The thought kept him from worrying about how furious Tink would be when they met. He hadn't seen Tink the night before; now it would be another full day before he saw him. He was excited, but a little disappointed. He had planned to patch up the Kinderhook boat and take it back up river, if he could get the day off.

Once their hasty meal was over and their equipment had been checked, Sergeant Cummings hustled them away from the fire and led them at a fast, silent pace to Malta Island. As they reached the river, it was Adam, looking at the Delaware, who made the first comment. Gazing at the dark river, he said, "Ain't like the water back home. No tang to it, and no swell to it. Just slides along and you wouldn't even know it was water unless you fell into it."

Joel Wedge and Jonas Tewksbury were on guard duty. Matt knew Jonas well. In Marblehead the guard tied up at the same dock at which Matt's lobster boat was moored. He spoke to Matt.

"Where's that deer I heard you got yesterday, Matt?

Do you think, maybe, I'll get a slice of it? After all, me and you are practically shipmates."

The request made Matt feel good. "It isn't all mine," he said. "But when I get my share, I guess most everybody in the company will get some." Matt looked up and down the river edge for the Kinderhook boat, but he couldn't find it in the dark.

The Sergeant called Adam and Matt to the bank. "This is the boat we'll take," he said. "Adam, you'll do the rowing. Matt, watch me. This is how we muffle oars so they can't be heard over a few yards away." He produced a piece of cloth, and using the flickering light from the guards' fire to see by, he wrapped it around an oarlock. "Now you do the other," he said, handing Matt some of the material.

Matt took it without a word. Who did the Sergeant think he was? There wasn't a boy in Marblehead who didn't know how to muffle oars when he was just about walking age.

Adam rowed them straight across the river to the New Jersey side, and when they could make out the jagged outline of the trees against the faintly lightening sky, they worked downstream. Once they stopped to listen to the creak of oars slowly passing them. "About six men rowing," whispered Adam.

"Sounds like a Durham boat, on patrol," answered the Sergeant. "It's on the other side of the river."

They started again, slowly, and when they could finally distinguish objects in the morning light, they floated in to shore, hid the boat in an alder thicket, and moved forward through the brush till they reached the river road that wound from McKonkey's Ferry to Trenton. The Sergeant advanced alone and scanned the road carefully in each direction. Then he signaled the others and they joined him. A dog started to bark. They stood silent, waiting.

For the first time Matt realized that they might be in some danger. He felt a little strange. Now he knew that marching wasn't the only thing that happened in war. He was glad that it was Sergeant Cummings and Adam Bean who were with him.

When the dog stopped barking, the Sergeant said softly, "There's a dozen farms between here and Trenton and we're planning to miss all of them. We'll go in a way and work down behind them through the woods. Keep a weather eye out for landmarks, so we come back to this spot. I'll go ahead, you next, Matt, and then Adam. Let's keep a dozen or so yards apart. That will give the others a chance to get away if one of us is taken."

If one of us is taken, thought Matt. He gulped a breath of air.

For an hour or more they picked their way through the cold, still woods, always quiet, always alert, watching for any sign of the enemy, careful to remember this large tree, this small clearing, or this stump or rock as a guide for their return. Occasionally smoke in the distance, a brook, or an open field seen through the trees changed their course a little, but always they bore southeast, slowly, cautiously.

It was midmorning when Sergeant Cummings signaled the men to join him. He was at the edge of a field where the road in the distance was visible. There was a fire at the roadside and about it lounged three figures.

"You can hardly see those black uniforms against the trees," whispered the Sergeant. "If it wasn't for the fire I'd have missed them. They're from Knyphausen's Regiment."

Matt could scarcely believe that he was looking at men who would capture him or even take his life if given the chance.

"We'll circle farther inland," said the Sergeant. "We'll have to keep a sharper lookout from now on. There might be Hessians out anywhere from here to Trenton."

They did circle inland and for a while Matt picked out every step he took. What if he made a noise by tripping over a root or breaking a fallen branch? Would the sound bring the enemy charging down on them?

The sun was noon high when Cummings waited for Matt and Adam to join him. Then, posting Adam as lookout on a low ridge overlooking the narrow ribbon of road in the distance, he directed Matt into a small gully where the sun spattered down through bare trees and the breeze forgot to nip at them. Here he signaled that they were to rest and eat.

The Sergeant did not speak but ate from his knapsack, and when he was finished he took Adam's place. Adam, too, was like the Sergeant; he said nothing. Matt felt a little secure for the first time since they had crossed the river road. He was thinking how comfortable it was to be in the shelter, when the Sergeant slid in beside them.

"There's a squad of Hessians moving up," he said. "Let's take a look at them."

The men left the gully and eased up to the top of the ridge. In the distance the men the Sergeant had spied looked like toy soldiers.

"Don't know where they're going," said Cummings. "Maybe to relieve some pickets. We're all right as long as they keep to the road. Matt, you take over; I'll rest a bit with Adam. Let us know if they swing off the road toward us."

Matt took over, scarcely daring to breathe as he watched the squad, looking almost ant-size as they moved along. He followed them with his eyes till they disappeared behind a line of trees. What if something happened that he should see but didn't? He remained staring at the road down which the Hessians had traveled, hardly daring to move a finger. He almost jumped when the Sergeant and Adam crept up beside him.

"All quiet?" asked Cummings.

Matt nodded his head.

"Good work, Matt," said Adam.

"We ought to see Trenton soon, now," announced the Sergeant. "Let's move along."

Matt noticed that the Sergeant did not commend him for his work. He never did.

In less than an hour they were crouched behind a fallen tree looking at Trenton.

"Not a redoubt or a trench anywhere," whispered Adam.

"And very few pickets about," added Cummings. "They must be guarding the river side more than the land side."

"Just look at that town," said Adam. "Outside of a few soldiers and a few baggage wagons, you'd never know there was an army down there."

"They're there all right," commented the Sergeant. "Those wandering around with the blue uniforms are Rall's Grenadiers. He's in command. Those in the red uniforms are Alt Lossburgers."

"How'd you like to have a uniform like one of them, Matt?"

"Rather have one of those places to sleep in," Matt answered. His voice was a little strained. He was wondering how long they would stay there. He wished he was back in camp.

Sergeant Cummings was in no hurry. He pointed out the solid stone barracks, the blacksmith shop, the church, the tannery, and watched the goings and comings in the town for an hour. Finally he said, "I guess we've got all we want to know. Let's get back to the boat."

Quietly they slipped away from their hidden vantage point and moved back to the hollow in which they had rested. Here they ate what morsels were left in their knapsacks.

They had marked their route well and worked through the woods by the exact course on which they had come. The only difference they noted on the return trip was that the three pickets about the fire had changed from men in black to men in red, the Alt Lossburgers having relieved the Knyphausens.

"Haven't seen a thing but the pickets," said Cummings. "We've been lucky so far."

61

It was Adam who raised his hand for quiet as they paused at the road's edge for the dash across it to the boat. "There's someone over there," he whispered.

The men froze, listening. Then it came. There was someone between them and the boat. Matt's heart started pounding.

"Wait here," ordered the Sergeant, "and if I'm not back in half an hour, go up this side of the river to McKonkey's and cross over there—if you can make it."

He wasn't gone more than five minutes when he rejoined them. "There's only one of them," he said. "I think he's a Tory and I think he's found our boat."

"Is he armed?" asked Adam.

"No," the Sergeant replied. "All he has is a piece of rope. It's an old trick. If we catch him, he'll say he was looking for a lost cow. Matt, you and I will go down a hundred yards. Adam, you give us time to get there, and then cross the road into the woods and come quietly in our direction. We should catch him between us. Don't shoot unless there's no other way. We want to take him alive."

Matt wished, more than ever, that he was back in camp, even back home in Marblehead. He was trembling. He followed Sergeant Cummings, because it seemed the safest thing to do. Not for the world would he let his old schoolteacher get out of sight, now.

They were across the road, moving as stealthily as possible up through the woods to meet Adam, when they heard Adam shout. "I've got him!" His words were followed by the sound of thuds and wild thrashing about.

There was no effort to be quiet now. The Sergeant took off pell-mell toward the sound, with Matt at his heels.

They arrived in time to see Adam topple over backward. The man who sent him toppling turned on the advancing Sergeant and Matt. Matt stopped short, but the Sergeant charged ahead to be met with a wild swing from the man's clenched fist. The Sergeant's gun flew from his hands and he, too, like Adam, was flat on the ground. He was up in an instant charging again. This time it was the man who staggered back and into Adam's grasp. Desperately Adam locked the man's arms to his sides and held on like a vise till the Sergeant picked up his gun and leveled it at the man's chest.

The man suddenly lost his taste for battle. "It's all right, Sergeant, don't shoot. I've had aplenty. Faith, I wasn't doing a bit of harm except looking for a lost cow." He shook a length of rope. "And, this one," his head moved backward to indicate Adam, who still held him secure, "jumped on me back without a single word. Sure, and I meant no harm."

"Let him free," ordered Cummings. "Tie up his hands with his rope. The sound of this ruckus has probably carried all the way to Trenton. Matt, get down and untie the boat; it's just below here. You take the oars."

Matt rushed down to the water's edge and found the boat. How he wanted to get across the river. More than anything else he wanted to get across the river. It seemed to him that it was an age before the protesting captive crashed through the woods propelled by Adam, who was using the butt of his musket as a prod.

Matt, sitting nervously at the oars, held the boat against the bank.

"Into the bow, Adam, and keep your musket ready," ordered the Sergeant. He shoved the prisoner. "The stern for you, and don't make a false move."

The man half tumbled down the bank and into the stern as Adam scrambled up ahead.

"Now pull as you never pulled before, Matt," ordered Cummings as he took his seat beside the man.

If Matt hadn't been so frightened he would have laughed. The Sergeant and the captive each had an eye that was swelling and turning black.

"Pull, Matt, pull," urged Cummings. Matt pulled and watched the man seated beside the Sergeant. Long, lean, shabby. The eye that wasn't rapidly closing was a clear cold blue. The man started to protest again and his voice was filled with the brogue of Ireland.

The Sergeant cut him off. "Shut up," he said in a sharper voice than Matt had ever heard him use.

The man kept still and Cummings turned half about to watch the New Jersey shore. He had hardly turned when he shouted, "Here they come!"

Through the trees on the river's edge appeared four Hessians in red. One, who seemed to be the leader, shouted something that Matt didn't understand.

"Alt Lossburgers," announced Adam, and raised his musket.

Matt could see its barrel from the corner of his eye. Then came the deafening explosion. Matt's ears rang with it and he was choked with fumes and smoke. He barely heard Adam shout, "Missed! Pull the bottom out of the river, Matt!"

Matt pulled and watched as white smoke engulfed the

64

men on the shore. He heard the whir of musket balls hum over his head.

The Sergeant's gun exploded, and as he turned to reload, he shouted, "Upstream, Matt! Swing upstream!"

Matt's throat had gone dry, and his stomach seemed to have deserted him. As if he were in a dream, he obeyed the Sergeant and swung upstream.

"Now, back across," ordered Cummings.

Matt swung back. Adam's gun roared again. Matt, his ears ringing, knew his hearing was gone for good.

The cloud of smoke formed again on the opposite shore and Matt saw water spurt in little geysers at the spot where they would have been had he gone straight ahead. He was damp with sweat. He heard the Sergeant's gun again and was surprised that he heard it. He watched the men on the bank frantically reloading. They were getting smaller now. They fired again and the little geysers spurted up yards to the stern.

It was the man who had been looking for cows who spoke. "Ye can take it a little easier now, lad. Ye're out o' range."

Matt looked at him—at his thin face, at his good blue eye—and knew that he was looking at a man who hadn't been afraid. He knew, too, that the man had watched him and had marked him as someone who was scared.

Sergeant Cummings turned and his voice was a little tired. "Matt, slow down, but keep on pulling."

Adam spoke up. "Would have gotten one of 'em I expect if the boat had been held on a little steadier course."

10

THEY DIDN'T carry the prisoner all the way to Malta Island but pulled in at McKonkey's Ferry. "Matt," said the Sergeant, "we'll land this man here, and Adam and I will take him to Colonel Glover. He'll know what to do with him. You take the boat on up to the island."

Slowly Matt rowed the two miles up to Malta Island. As he pulled in toward shore, Joel Wedge and Jonas Tewksbury rushed down the bank to meet him.

"Tell us about it, Matt," they both exploded together. "Heard he pretty near killed the Sergeant and Adam."

Matt looked astounded. "Who pretty near killed the Sergeant and Adam?"

"The spy you caught over in Jersey. One of them Philadelphia Light Horses was here ten minutes ago and told us about it. He said he just came from McKonkey's and that he saw three Marbleheaders bring John Honeyman in," explained Jonas.

"John Honeyman?" said Matt, blankly.

"Sure, John Honeyman. The worst Tory spy in these parts," said Jonas.

"Did he put up the fight the Philadelphia dandy said he did?" asked Joel Wedge.

"We knew it was you and Adam and Cummings," added Jonas. "You're the only ones, except the patrol boats, that were out."

It was getting dark again and Matt was weary. He was surprised, too, that his legs could hold him up, they felt so weak.

Joel Wedge tied the boat up and gave Matt a pat on the back as they went up the river bank.

"Between shooting deer and catching spies, you'll be a hero yet, boy. Did he really put up the fight we heard about?"

"I've got to get back for roll call," said Matt. "Why don't you ask the Sergeant or Adam, when you're relieved?"

"Wait till we're relieved?" exploded Jonas. "Not when we got one of the men who did it right here. If you don't tell us, Matt, we'll sit on you till you do. Besides, didn't I tie up at the same wharf with you back home? Is that the way to treat someone who's been practically a shipmate for years? Matt, you've got to tell us. We're just beginning our night watch and we won't be free for hours."

Matt started reluctantly to tell the men of the events of the day, but as he progressed he was surprised to find himself enjoying it. It was something, he felt, to have two grown men listening carefully to every little word he said.

It was not until he was on his way again that he realized that, although it had not been his deliberate intention, he had given the men the impression that his part in the capture was much more than it had been. He had left them, somehow, with the thought that if he wasn't exactly a hero, he was pretty close to it.

When he reached camp the men were divided as to what was the more important, or which came first: the capture of John Honeyman, or Brad Ferguson standing guard over a side of venison in the middle of the company street.

Sam Nelson, the company butcher, standing by with a cleaver in one hand and a carving knife in the other, shouted as Matt approached.

"Tell this Indian that this is our meat. I've been waiting to break it down almost half the afternoon, but he won't let anyone near it till you say so."

"It's his," defended Brad. "Didn't him and me get it together?" He spoke to Matt. "There it is, boy," he said and pointed to the carcass. "What's this I hear about you and John Honeyman? Never will understand how anybody in boots like you're wearing could catch a man. He sure must have been stone deaf not to hear you when you were a mile away."

"Can I start cutting?" asked Sam.

"What about that spy you caught?" asked Jethro Hatch. "We been waitin' for the Sergeant and Adam to come up from headquarters to tell us, but they ain't here yet."

"Heard he put up a real battle," said Maillet, the teamster.

Others crowded around and for the second time since he had landed at Malta Island, Matt was the center of attention. It made him forget his weariness, and in its place grew a feeling of great importance.

"Cut up the deer, Sam," he said. His voice had weight to it. "And save some for the men on boat guard. I promised them a share."

"Along with a prime steak for the Colonel," added Sam.

68

"What about John Honeyman?" insisted Jethro. "Tell us about that while Sam's working."

Matt talked as the men waited for a portion of venison, and they listened as they skewered the meat on bayonet ends and set it sizzling in the fire. Then he retold the story as new men came up, and then he retold it again. And each time it was repeated, his part in the capture became a little more important. It was not until the Sergeant and Adam strode into camp that Matt realized how his story had expanded, for the men arrived just in time to hear Tink Cooper speak from the dim-lit edge of the crowd.

"Matt," he said, "yesterday you caught a deer; today you caught a spy. Tell us what you're going to do tomorrow, Matt."

Matt felt the bitterness in Tink's voice, but more than that, he knew how he must have sounded to the men. Tink's words gave him the sensation of being pushed off a boat dock into an ocean of cold, cold water.

The arrival of the Sergeant and Adam drew the attention of the men and they were showered with questions concerning the capture. As soon as he could manage it, Matt, red of face and ashamed, slipped away and crawled into his tent.

11

IN THE KEITH House where headquarters were established, John Honeyman stood in the center of a group of officers, looking coolly from one to the other and flatly refusing to answer any of the questions they poured at him. Singly, and in groups, the officers tried to pry information from him and it was not until their voices grew angry and threatening that General Washington stepped forward and spoke to his men.

"Gentlemen," he said, "it may be that this prisoner is abashed by so much attention. Perhaps it would be easier for him to speak if there were fewer of us here. I have a report from Colonel Glover covering the information gathered by the men who took Mr. Honeyman prisoner earlier today. I think, perhaps, that from this report I can ask him certain questions that he might find it to his advantage to answer. I only ask one consideration. That is that I might question him alone."

The officers looked at each other with amazement. "But, Sir . . ." one started to say.

"I know how you feel," interrupted the General, holding up his hand. "I think I know what you are going to say, but let me assure you that if I need any physical assistance, should the prisoner get, let us say, boisterous, I shall certainly be heard. Now, if you please."

The officers looked uncertainly at each other. There wasn't a man in the room who wouldn't have laid down his life for his Commander. They hesitated, then General Greene spoke, "We'll be near if you should need us, Sir." Slowly the men filed from the room, chagrined at John Honeyman's successful defiance and hopeful that their General would succeed where they had failed.

When the door was closed and the sound of the retreating men stilled, George Washington turned toward the prisoner with a look of pleasure on his face. "John Honeyman," he said, "if they only knew what they owe to you. I wondered if you would ever get here."

John Honeyman stepped forward and spoke, in his musical Irish voice. "Faith, General, it wasn't so hard as I expected. Pardon me for mentioning it but, although the boys you sent were fine lads, they were far easier to find than a bawling cow with a bell on each hoof. And by the same token, I had to almost bellow like a bull for them to find me."

"I considered that when we picked the Massachusetts fishermen for the job," said the General. "Now if we had sent some of my moccasined Virginians, you might not have been quite so successful." There was a half-smile on the General's face. "However, there is nothing wrong with the report the men turned in on the situation between here and Trenton. In fact, it is excellent, and I think they gave a good account of themselves once they found you."

"Sure, and I'll be the first one to agree to that," said John Honeyman, gingerly touching his swollen eye. "The next time I'll be a little less hard to capture. But then, ye're waiting to hear the bit of knowledge I have to add to their report."

George Washington spoke slowly. "As much as I dislike doing it, John, I must inform you of something before you start. When we have finished here, you will be transported to the guardhouse, and you will spend some time there before it will be made possible for you to return to Trenton. I'm indeed sorry, but there is no other way."

The prisoner smiled. "Sure, and I understand, sir. I, too, know there is no other way. Now, sir, I am ready for any of the questions ye have a mind to ask me, and perhaps I'll have a bit of information to add that may be of some help."

12

IT WAS LATE when Matt awoke. In spite of having been dog-tired he hadn't slept very well. He had made a fool of himself the night before with his story of the capture of John Honeyman, and he knew it. Why had he talked as though he had had a great deal to do with it, when all he did was row the boat away from the New Jersey side of the river? And he wouldn't have been able to do that as well as he had if he hadn't been so scared. Tink's remark certainly showed him up for what he was. As he thought it over, he was glad Tink had done it. It had kept him from making a bigger fool of himself. It wouldn't have taken long before the men about the camp realized he was just talking, if they didn't realize it already. He was glad of one thing, and that was that Brad Ferguson had left the campfire after the first telling. That story hadn't been so bad as he remembered it.

He crawled out from beneath his blanket. He knew what he was going to do. He was going down to the Second Company and tell Tink he was ready to go. The men might not find out that he didn't shoot the deer; they might not find out how little he had to do with the capture of John Honeyman, but they would find out, as soon as fighting began, that he was afraid. He wasn't going to let that happen.

When he came from his tent Adam was the only man about. Matt watched him hobble to a small pile of wood, reach down, pick up a chunk, and hobble back to the fire.

He turned as he heard Matt. "Stiff as a board," he said. "Just can't take the kind of treatment that Tory gave out any more."

Matt walked to the fire and took the food Adam offered —a piece of hard bread and a bowl of thin gruel. He ate silently, close to the fire. It seemed that every day was a little colder than the day before. He had heard Sergeant Cummings say that ice a foot thick would support an army. If it kept as cold as this, it wouldn't be long till the Delaware was solid all the way over. Only last night two men at the fire said they had crossed the river on the ice above Easton only a day ago. If it was frozen solid above Easton, which wasn't very far north, it wouldn't be long until the icy edges at McKonkey's Ferry reached out and met in the middle of the river, and once they met, the ice would grow thicker and thicker until the Hessians could cross and. . . . He stopped thinking about it. He'd find Tink and tell him that as soon as he took the Kinderhooks' boat back, they could start for the Massachusetts coast where they belonged.

Adam, who was hanging up his blankets in the cold air, shook his head soberly as Matt rose from the fire and without a word walked down the company street.

A cook of the Second Company, scouring an iron pot with sand, stopped long enough to point out the tent in which Tink slept.

"He ain't up yet," said the man. "You got to pull him out of bed every morning and at that it ain't worth the effort. He don't do nothing he ain't forced to do, and then he spends all his time sulking about it. Whatever made him think he was a soldier? He's a lot different from you, boy, scouting all the way to Trenton and helping to capture that Honeyman. I was up to your end of the camp last night and heard you tell about it. Do me a favor, will you? When you wake him up,"—he jerked his thumb toward Tink's tent—"tell him to get his own breakfast. I've got to go up to the mill and argue for our company's flour ration."

Matt walked to the tent and slipped in beside Tink. As the cook had said, Tink was fast asleep. Matt leaned over and shook him. "Tink," he whispered, "Tink."

Tink rolled over, opened his eyes, screwed up his face, and squinted at Matt. Then he mumbled, "What are you doing here?"

Matt hesitated before he answered, "If you want to leave, I'll go with you."

Tink sat up. He wasn't very enthusiastic. "Oh," he said, "so you want to leave. I thought we were going to leave two or three days ago?"

"I guess I've been busy," answered Matt, lamely.

"Busy being a hero," snapped Tink. "I'll tell you something. I'm leaving today whether you are or not." He rose and his voice became sarcastic. "Do you want to go right this instant or can I get something to eat first?"

Matt hesitated again, "There is something I have to do: I've got a boat to take up the river—the one I brought the deer down in. As soon as I take it back, we'll get away."

75

"Take a boat up the river?" Tink gave a hard little laugh. "It's always something, isn't it, Matt? Forget it, I'll leave by myself."

"Listen, Tink," Matt said, hastily. "I borrowed the boat; I've got to take it back."

"Can't you get someone else to do it?" said Tink.

"No," Matt answered.

Tink thought a minute before he spoke again. "Can you be back by noon?"

"I think so," said Matt.

"Do you know what?" Tink sounded more eager. "I've got two horses to watch up in the pasture beyond the New Jersey Militia Camp. You meet me there, and we won't have to walk away from here. We'll take the horses and ride."

"Take the horses?" questioned Matt.

"Sure, we'll take the horses. We'll be miles away from here before anyone knows it."

"But that's stealing," protested Matt.

"What of it?" snapped Tink. "I've stolen before. Remember the Portuguese spyglass we used to take out lobstering? I took it and sold it the night before we left Marblehead. Where did you think I got the money we spent coming down here? That's why we got to go to Salem or Gloucester or someplace. I can't go home."

Matt's mouth dropped open. What was it Adam Bean had said as they were marching to McKonkey's Ferry? Tink Cooper must have done something to leave in such a hurry.

When Matt recovered his speech, he said dully, "I'm not taking a horse."

"Afraid?" said Tink.

Matt paused again. Was he afraid? He seemed to be afraid of everything. He was afraid of Tink right now. "I don't know," he said, very low. "But, afraid or not, I'm not taking a horse that doesn't belong to me."

"In a minute you'll be backing out entirely," said Tink. "If you back out this time, do you know what I'm going to do? I'm going to whip the daylights out of you. You can't keep calling me a friend and not keep your promises, and you promised me more than once that you'd leave here. Now, are you going or aren't you going?" He stepped so close to Matt that Matt felt Tink's breath on his upturned face.

"I said I was going," answered Matt, not daring to look into Tink's eyes. Then he was surprised to hear Tink laugh.

"All right, Matty, my boy," he said. "We won't take the horses. But you be up at the pasture by noon with what you need in a knapsack, and in a week's time, horses or no horses, we'll be back where we belong."

13

AS MATT WALKED to Malta Island to get the Kinderhooks' boat, he found it hard to believe that he was going to leave camp with Tink at noontime. He found it hard to believe, too, that he hadn't been very much upset or shocked when he learned that Tink had taken the Portuguese spyglass. The Kinderhook boat seemed much more important to him at this time.

As he came down the path to the river where Tom Brimblecom and Zeb Lacy were guarding the boats, they rose from the husky little fire that was keeping them warm and Tom spoke almost before Matt reached them.

"Say, did you see that Adam, this morning? He looked like he was keelhauled. Honeyman certainly gave him a rough time of it."

Matt nodded. "Adam's sort of lame, all right." Then quickly he added, "I came down here for the boat I borrowed to bring the deer down the river."

The men didn't want to change the subject, right now. "Sergeant Cummings got his, too," said Zeb. "What an eye! It looks as if someone had poked an oar into it. You were lucky you didn't get banged up the way they did."

Matt said nothing. He knew why he didn't get banged up.

Tom took up the conversation. "Wouldn't surprise me a bit if we were all mustered out to watch a hangin' any day now. They sure ain't goin' to let that Tory loose again."

Matt turned to look at the boats lined up in the narrow passageway between the shore and Malta Island. Even in Marblehead he had never seen so many boats at one time. The Pennsylvania men had scoured the river to get them. Flat, shallow bateaux, stubby rowboats, long, deep-floating Durham boats, used in times of peace to haul iron ore down from the Pennsylvania mines to the forges about Philadelphia. The Durham boats when propelled by six or eight rowers were capable of carrying the heaviest of loads. Among them he picked out the boat that belonged to the Kinderhooks. "That's the boat I want, down there," he said.

"Boat?" said Tom. "What boat you talkin' about?"

Matt pointed. "That one there." He looked again. "Say, it isn't leaking."

Tom followed the direction of Matt's finger. "Oh, that one. It's the smallest boat we got, and of course it isn't leaking. Jethro Hatch caulked it with pine pitch yesterday."

Matt shrugged. "I guess that saves me a job. I'm going to take it up river to the people who let me borrow it." He started down the bank.

"Wait, wait, hold up!" shouted Tom. "You got a paper?"

Matt turned. "A paper?"

"Yep. A paper from John Glover saying you can take the boat."

79

"I don't have to have a paper from Colonel Glover," said Matt. "I rowed that boat here. I can take it."

"Not without a paper from John Glover, you can't," said Tom.

Zeb came over. "You talking about the boat Hatch patched up yesterday?"

"Yep," said Tom.

Zeb snorted. "That's one boat he ain't taking. Jethro told me Colonel John and General Washington himself were here, and the General pointed out that very boat and said, 'It looks like a real light skiff. I may be needing it soon. Don't let it get away.' Jethro told me those were his very words."

"Guess that settles that," said Tom.

"But it's my boat," protested Matt. "I didn't bring it here to keep the Hessians from getting it. I only borrowed it...."

"Now, Matt," interrupted Tom. "You don't have to go wasting any words on us. And don't start no fuss. Just go get a paper from the Colonel, or maybe General Washington, and the boat's yours. But as long as it's behind Malta Island and we're guarding it, you can stew and fret as much as you want, but it won't do you a bit of good. Now, if you want to sit a spell and talk, we'd like to have you, but unless you got a paper, we don't want to hear any more about that boat."

Matt stood still while the two men returned to the fire and squatted down beside it.

"Come on, Matt," invited Zeb. "Stay awhile. You'll probably get the boat as soon as the General is finished with it. No sense in getting all worked up about it."

"You'd get worked up," snapped Matt, "if you borrowed a boat and promised to return it and then couldn't get it."

"Guess I would," said Zeb, easily. "But I know what I'd do. I'd go to the folks I borrowed it from and tell them I'd bring it back as soon as I could. I wouldn't want them to think I stole it."

"That's the same thing I'd do," added Tom Brimblecom. "Tell 'em it ain't your fault that the army's bigger than you are."

"Just stick around." Zeb laughed. "The way a lot of these men are pulling out on the sly and scootin' for home like scared salmon, it won't be long before the army won't be any bigger than you are, then you can get your boat and there won't be anyone to stop you."

Matt's face grew a deep crimson. He started to say something but thought better of it. What did these two know about the men who left the army to go home? Those who left had problems of their own, didn't they? They were cold all the time, and hungry all the time, and maybe—he hesitated in his thoughts—maybe some were scared all the time, too. If a man was scared all the time, wouldn't it be better for him to leave and let those who weren't scared stay and fight? A scared man would only be in the way, anyhow.

He turned aside till the color left his face. Then he said, almost bitterly, "I'm going."

On the way to the Kinderhooks', four men from the New Jersey Militia on picket duty two miles from camp stopped him. The corporal, when Matt had reported his name and regiment, stepped toward him. "Matt Doliber," he repeated. "You're one of them as caught John Honeyman, ain't you? Boys," he said to the others, "this is one of them Marblehead men who caught Honeyman." He turned back to Matt. "We been chasin' that Tory all over Jersey for months and you come down from Massachusetts and, I guess, don't hardly know your way around, and you catch him right away." He held out his hand. "Shake." He solemnly shook hands. "Heard all about it last night. Did he put up the fight they all say he did?"

Matt looked at the other men, then said, "He put up a pretty good fight."

"Heard a couple of your men were beat up pretty good," continued the guard. "That Honeyman's a corker, all right, but now we got him, I guess as soon as they find out what they want to know from him, they'll hang him from the highest tree on this side of the river. Say, you can go through this post any time you want." Then he laughed. "Ain't planning on bringing back another spy, are you? There's more almost as bad as him running around."

Matt shook his head. "No, I guess I wouldn't want to tackle another one, not alone, anyways."

As he walked on down the road he could have bitten his tongue. Here he was again making folks believe he had taken a great hand in the capture of John Honeyman. He knew it was wrong. He'd be glad when this afternoon came and he got away with Tink.

82

14

IT WASN'T hard to find the Kinderhook farm sitting across the road from the river. It looked different from the last time he had been there. The spot on the bank where the boat had been hidden in the willows looked especially empty when he passed. He wished that he had wanted to come.

As he turned into the farmyard, Fritz, the dog, gave a halfhearted warning to those inside and retreated. The door swung open and Paula gazed coolly at him. Pudgy Mr. Kinderhook peered over her shoulder.

"Oh, Mobblehedt," he said.

"I've got something to explain," said Matt, lamely.

"You certainly have," said Paula, "and I hope you can explain it better than he can." Her yellow braids bobbed as she looked over her shoulder toward the room behind her.

"Yes," said Mr. Kinderhook. "Come in und eggs-plain."

How did they know he hadn't the boat, thought Matt. They couldn't see from the kitchen whether he had rowed or walked. Before he was half over the threshold, a voice he knew greeted him.

"If you know anything about the fence, tell them."

Brad Ferguson, sitting uncomfortably on the long bench beside the fire, looked as miserable as it was possible for him to look.

"The fence?" said the surprised Matt as the door closed behind him.

"The fence," said Brad. "Here I come up with a little venison as a present and they think I stole their fence."

"We didn't say you took the fence," said Paula. "We just asked if you know who took it."

"No, ve don't blame on you the fence," added Klaus Kinderhook. "Und if ve did, it's gone." He held his hands apart chest high in a gesture of hopelessness. "It von't come back. Maybe speaking to somebody about it, you vere? Maybe...." His voice trailed off.

"I didn't mention it to anyone," said Brad. "I forgot it was there."

Matt peered out through the window. The fence they had crossed with the deer was gone, every post and rail. He looked from Mr. Kinderhook to Paula. He knew nothing about the fence, and he had to explain about the boat after this. He grew red. The boat—he had to tell them about the boat. How warm it was in the house. He'd give anything just to sit awhile and soak up the warmth, but how could he stay? He was thoroughly miserable. Hardly hearing his own voice, he blurted out, "I didn't bring the boat back. The army wants to keep it. I'll bring it back as soon as I can. I'd better go now."

Brad jumped up. "I've got to mosey along, too," he said.

"Boys, boys," almost shouted Mr. Kinderhook. "Paula und me don't mean nothings by the fence talk. Ve iss sorry to lose it, the fence, but ve don't mean nothings. You stay here und Paula makes snitz pie mittoudt yellow apples." He spoke to Paula but pointed at Brad. "Didn't he bring venison ve don't have since Mels left?"

"Yes, Papa," said Paula, but she looked at Matt. "He didn't bring the boat back, Mels' boat."

"No, he don't bring it back, but he comes to tell us. He don't have to do that," said Paula's father. He directed his words toward Matt.

"Come, you und me ve sit close by the fire und talk about Mobblehedt. You," he pointed at Brad, "go by the cellar und get apples for the snitz. Paula, you tell him ver. Snitz iss like venison; I don't have it all vinter."

For a long time Matt sat dejectedly near the fire listening to Klaus Kinderhook, answering his questions without thinking too much, and stealing glances at Paula as she sifted, kneaded, rolled, and cut, while Brad, silent for once, sat and watched almost at her elbow. When the pie was slid into the oven, Paula made a serious business of cleaning up the remains, sweeping a speck of flour dust from the floor and scouring the utensils she had used in the pie making. As she worked she became more agreeable, and by the time she had finished she was laughing with Brad, as she had done on the first visit, and he was now bubbling over with talk.

It was Fritz, the dog, who interrupted them, this time not with the weary, dutiful bark that had greeted Matt, but with an excited yip and a long, deep growl that sent Paula flying to the window. "Papa," she said excitedly, "it's the Seaveys."

Papa lurched up. "Ach, no, not the Seaveys." He

turned and quickly explained to Matt. "Everyone by the Delaware iss Englishers but us. Und those that are Tories, I can't count them, but the Seaveys, ach, they iss the vorst. Come from the vindow, Paula. I vill go out und talk to them. You boys stay by the kitchen."

Brad sprang up and seized his rifle. "They ain't nothin' worse than Tories. I'll go with you."

"No, no, no," Klaus Kinderhook sputtered. "Troubles mitt the Seaveys, I don't vant. I talk alone to them." The farmer went through the door as fast as his bulk would let him.

Brad patted his rifle and addressed it. "Guess we'll be missing a little fun sitting in here all quiet, and only three of them out there with just two guns between them." He looked at Matt. "You and me could take care of them if we wanted to."

"Mr. Kinderhook said we were to stay here," said Matt. His voice sounded a little weak.

Paula added, hastily, "Yes, Papa wants us to stay here. Papa doesn't want trouble with the local folks."

"I'll stay here," agreed Brad, "but if they start anything, I reckon I'd like to help finish it."

"Maybe there won't be any trouble," said Matt.

Brad turned. "Hey, you don't sound like the soldier that helped bring in John Honeyman."

Matt flushed.

Paula looked at Brad, her eyes wide. "Has John Honeyman been captured?"

"Sure," answered Brad. "And Matt over there was one of them that did it."

Paula turned toward Matt. "You didn't?" Amazement made her voice sound husky. "Why, John Honeyman is the very worst Tory and spy and, and. . . ." Her excitement smothered her words.

Matt sat miserably staring at the floor.

"When did it happen? How did you do it? Was he real hard to catch?" Paula's questions came one upon the other.

Brad, watching carefully from a window, said, "Say, there's some kind of argument going on, and it looks like your Papa is telling them a thing or two."

"I do hope he doesn't lose his temper," said Paula. She forgot her excitement about John Honeyman to look through the window.

Matt was relieved. Brad had saved him this time, whether he knew it or not. He wished he could get away. He'd better get away soon if he wanted to meet Tink Cooper at noon.

"They're going," announced Paula.

"And they ain't too happy about it," added Brad. They both peered from the window until the sound of Klaus Kinderhook's foot was on the stoop and the door swung open.

Mr. Kinderhook, his round cheeks red with the cold and excitement, came in, walked to the bench, and sank down beside Matt.

"Mobblehedt," he said, "it iss good you did not bring back the boat. The Seaveys, that's vot they vanted, to cross the river, my Mels' boat, but I tell them the boat iss by McKonkey's mitt General Washington. They said

General Washington had every boat on the river, und how did he expect honest citizens to get over to New Jersey. You know vy they vant to go by New Jersey? The first thing you know they iss in Trenton telling Colonel Rall of something they know." He patted Matt on the knee. "Good it iss, boy, you did not bring back the boat."

"Papa," said Paula, "do you know who was captured?"

"Captured?" asked her father.

"Yes, captured," said Paula. "John Honeyman." She couldn't keep the news back.

"John Honeyman?" Klaus Kinderhook repeated.

"Yes, John Honeyman," echoed Paula. "And who do you think caught him?"

The farmer's jowls flapped as he shook his head. "I don't know."

"Beside you sitting, he is!" exclaimed Paula, and she stamped her foot as she did the night she helped Matt put the boat in the water. "He's sitting beside you," she corrected.

Paula's father was almost as excited as she. He looked steadily at Matt and said, "Him? Mobblehedt?"

"Yes," answered Paula. "Him. Mobblehedt." Then she laughed a tinkling little laugh and turned almost scarlet.

Klaus Kinderhook rose and went to a cupboard and got out a long-stemmed clay pipe. Without a word he filled it and lit it with a splinter he kindled in the fire. He sat back and blew out a white cloud of smoke and said gravely, "Me, I am sorry I talk about the fence. Nobody steals the fence. Maybe General Washington's men come by the

88

fence und maybe borrow it, but nobody steals the fence. I give it to them. Even if they don't know I give it to them, I give it to them." He sat solidly back leaning against the wall. Then suddenly he sat upright. "No, I don't give it to them. Ve give it to them. Me und Paula, ve give it to them."

15

FILLED WITH snitz pie and milk and warm all the way through, Matt and Brad walked down the long wooded road that led from the Kinderhook farm. Neither spoke for a mile, covering the ground in easy strides, each thinking his own thoughts. Matt, about Paula Kinderhook. He didn't understand her. She had hardly said a dozen words to him, yet this time she gave him the largest slice of pie and the biggest mug of milk. The mug was decorated in all sorts of colors and around the edge was written *Wenn Sie einsam sind, ist unser Haus Ihres*. Brad had noticed the words and asked what it meant, but Paula was busy and had not answered. She must have heard him for when her father chuckled, she turned her head away and didn't look back for a long while.

Matt would remember those words and the odd-looking jammed-together curlycued letters that made them. He repeated them to himself, *"Wenn Sie einsam sind, ist unser Haus Ihres."* If he found someone who could speak the language Klaus Kinderhook spoke, he'd find out what it meant.

They were climbing a low grade that gave them a view of the river, black and smooth, through the leaf-bare trees, when Brad spoke.

"Did you ever hear such a fuss about a rail fence? Good thing you didn't tell them who took it, or we'd never have gotten that pie."

Matt was startled. "Me, how could I tell them who took it?"

"It was you Massachusetts men, wasn't it?" answered Brad.

"Massachusetts men?" Matt's surprise was real.

"Sure," said Brad easily. "Saw the rails up at the far end of your area when I was bringing down the deer meat."

"At the end of our area?"

"Sure."

Matt thought for a minute. "I haven't been up there in a day or two. That's where Colonel Knox's artillery is."

"That's right. That's where I saw the rails. They aren't there now, though. I think they moved them down near the river. That's what I heard."

"Why didn't you tell the Kinderhooks?"

Brad shrugged. "Didn't know if they were the Kinderhook rails, even. Then, when you came, I thought you would tell them."

"I said I didn't even know about them," answered Matt.

Brad grinned. "Wal, I guess what they don't know won't hurt them. They couldn't get them back anyway." Then, as an afterthought, he asked, "Why did you come all the way up to tell them about the boat?"

Matt didn't answer and Brad spoke again. "Some things I don't understand about you. You come all the way up river to tell somebody you can't bring their boat back; yet when a little trouble starts, like them Seaveys coming, you sit in the corner like you was scared to death to let a peep out of you. We could have had us a time if we'd a-went out with Papa. I don't like to say this, but from the way you acted when the Seaveys came, I can't see you capturing John Honeyman. We should have had it out with those Tories, right there."

Matt didn't look at Brad. He took several strides before he spoke. "I didn't have very much to do with catching Honeyman. Sergeant Cummings and Adam Bean did it." He paused. "I just happened to be along with them." His voice was low and dismal. "Everybody asks me about it, like everybody asked me about shooting the deer. I guess maybe I talk too big. I really didn't have much to do with either."

Brad looked at Matt till Matt raised his head, then their eyes met. "Say," Brad drawled, "how long you been in this war? I mean, how long you been doin' actual fighting?"

Matt hesitated. This boy's eyes were clear and there was nothing in them that expressed scorn, or derision, or pity. Instantly he thought, as he had felt all along, here was someone with whom he could talk. Slowly he said, "I've been in the army almost a month, I guess, and I haven't done any fighting. All I've ever done is details, and march, and row back John Honeyman."

Brad didn't laugh. "You never shot at the middle of those white cross belts on a Redcoat's uniform?"

"I never shot at anything but the deer you killed; and I missed that."

"You ever been shot at?"

"When I was rowing back Honeyman."

92

Then Brad laughed. "Kind of made you sick and hot in your belly, didn't it?"

Matt hesitated again before answering. "Yes, I guess that's sort of the way I felt."

Brad laughed again. "You should have seen me the fust time I heard a ball screaming over my head. I turned and passed that ball like it was nailed in the middle of the air. Ran till I was out of breath so bad I just fell over and lay there. I had plenty of company, too."

Matt looked at Brad. He couldn't believe what the Virginian said.

"You mean you ran?" It was impossible; this boy wouldn't run from anything.

"That's 'cause I didn't have wings," answered Brad, cheerfully.

"Do you always run?" asked Matt.

"Nope," said Brad. "Just that once. Since then, I've been doin' an orderly retreat like everyone else. That don't mean I ain't scared, though. I ain't *not* scared, either. I'm kind of down the middle, in between. War-ring is like anything else. I guess it gets to be a job, just like rowin' boats is your job. You ain't scared out in a boat, are you?"

"No, I don't know as there's anything to be scared of," said Matt.

"That's where you're wrong," said Brad. "Don't you hear all the time about people drownin'?"

Matt spoke slowly. "My father drowned, but that doesn't make me afraid."

"See?" said Brad, as if he had won a great point. "See? I never had anybody drown I know of, but I sure get sick in the middle when I'm on the water. You want to know something? Rafe Davis and Jeff Conley had to just about hogtie me and sit on me to get me over to Long Island and back. Made my mind up then that if there wasn't no bridges I wasn't goin' to fight any more. And I ain't."

For the first time Matt was on the offensive side. "The ocean's pretty bad in a gale," he said. "That's how my father was lost off the Grand Banks, but a river"—he pointed to the Delaware—"isn't anything to be afraid of."

"Nothin' to be afraid of if you can swim like a rat, but I can't swim like a rat," said Brad. "You know, in a battle, if someone shoots at you, you got a chance of shootin' back if you ain't hit and yore powder's dry, but there's nothing you can do in water."

"You can grab something that floats and hang on, and if you don't get excited you're safe enough. What are you going to do if we have to cross the Delaware and fight?" Matt asked.

"What are you going to do, after you get across?" countered Brad.

Then Matt remembered. He wasn't going to cross the Delaware and fight. Right now he was on his way to meet Tink, and they were leaving. He stole a glance at Brad.

Brad, who had been watching the river as he walked, turned to him. "I sure wish they'd build a bridge across it. I'd sure like a crack at those Trenton Hessians before they drive us into the Allegheny Mountains. I hate to be fightin' with my back against the wall all the time. Makes me think of a little black snake. Get one out in the open and start pesterin' it and it runs like blazes; but you get it in a corner, and it'll turn and fight like it's crazy. You know, anybody can fight when his back is up against the wall. It's when a man has a choice of runnin' or fightin' and he stays and fights, that's what makes him a soldier." He paused for a moment. "You know, sometimes I wish I had a choice of goin' or not goin' in a boat. I ain't crossed a river in this war that somebody didn't make me. Maybe someday I might cross one by myself without any-one forcin' me."

16

MATT WAS late. It was past noon when he entered the lower end of the field in which Tink was acting as grass guard. Tink had hobbled the two horses he was watching and, side by side, they moved, nibbling at the sparse dead grass already nuzzled by dozens of other horses before them. Tink was sprawled on a blanket in a far corner of the field. He rose and shouted as Matt approached.

"It's about time you got here. I thought you were never coming."

Matt didn't speak, but came across the field. Tink kept talking as Matt came toward him.

"I thought you were never coming. I've got another blanket hidden behind a stump in the next field." Then he realized that Matt carried nothing but his musket.

"Where's your knapsack?" he questioned.

Matt stopped in front of Tink. He spoke slowly and clearly. "Tink, I'm not going." It seemed strange to Matt, but for the first time he was not afraid of offending Tink by anything he said or did.

Tink's voice became brittle. "Not going? You told me this morning you were going!"

Matt knew that for a long time he had led Tink into

believing he was going to run away with him. This morning, especially, he had promised, but now he didn't want to leave and he didn't want Tink to leave. Slowly he said, "I know I said I'd like to leave, Tink, but I don't want to go now. What I was hoping was that you would stay here, too."

"Is it because I said we'd take the horses?" asked Tink. "We don't have to take the horses. I told you that."

"No," answered Matt. "That's not it. I'm just not going."

Tink stared at him, then he barked, "You must be crazy staying in a place like this! Cold all the time. Hardly any food, and somebody always telling you what to do. You must be crazy or. . . ." He stopped, and as if he had discovered something, he started all over again. "I know what it is! Just because you helped catch that Tory and everybody is talking about it, you think you're a hero! Too good for your old friends, that's it, isn't it? Do you know what I'm going to do, right now? I'm going to show you how much of a hero you really are. I'm going to give you the thrashing of your life. I promise you that. If there is anything I hate it's a friend that turns against you for no reason, except he did something big. I don't care if you stay here and rot. I'm sure going to make you remember me." He clenched his fists and took a step forward. "Now you're going to get it."

Matt couldn't believe that he stood unflinching in front of Tink, nor did he recognize his own voice as he said, "I wouldn't try it, if I were you."

If he had hit Tink with his musket butt he couldn't have stopped him any quicker. Tink's mouth dropped open, and he stared unbelievingly down at Matt. Then his eyes fell and the threat was gone from his voice. "I guess I can remember when we were friends," he mumbled. "That's the reason I'm going to let you go." He stepped back.

If Matt was surprised at his own actions up to this point, he was more surprised than ever when he insisted, "Don't let that stop you, Tink. If you want to whip me you've got the right to try."

Tink continued to step back. "I ain't got time to fight," he growled. "I'm leaving, and I'm leaving alone. Nobody in his right mind would stay in a place like this. I'm going, and I'll tell you, Master Hero, it's good riddance." He walked away grumbling to himself toward the horses that had inched along almost to the road.

Matt walked alongside Tink. He wouldn't be shaken off. He didn't want Tink to leave.

He tried again. "Why don't you change your mind, Tink?" he pleaded. "We could be together. . . ."

Tink turned on him. He was white with fury. He sputtered his words. "You think I'll stay just because you asked me, don't you? Well, I'm not staying. I wouldn't do anything you said, if it killed me. I never did do anything you said and I'm not going to start now. You go on back to your company and sit and wait and see how long it is till you hear from me again." He reached down and picked up a stick and Matt watched him as he charged viciously at the startled horses.

17

THERE WAS unusual activity about General Washington's headquarters. At intervals all morning long, couriers had arrived and swung off lathered horses, quickly passed the guard, and reappeared, to remount slowly and sag with fatigue in the saddle. Occasionally a fresh courier arrived for instructions, received them, and came scurrying out the door, and his horse was off and running as the rider's foot hit the stirrup.

Then the regimental commanders and the aides came; singly and in groups they arrived, their closely drawn capes and greatcoats covering uniforms of regiments from New Hampshire to Virginia. The uniforms, primarily blue, were decorated in a rainbow of brave colors—reds, greens, yellows, browns, buffs. Each officer upon arrival made his way to the dining hall, warmed front and back before the crackling fire in the hearth, and took his place at the long table that marched down the center of the room.

It was late afternoon and the last of the officers had been warmed and was seated when General Washington formally opened the meeting. He stood, tall and calm, at the head of the table. A sheaf of messages was before him.

He placed beside them a rolled map he had been studying. He let his gaze fall on each man in turn: men who were not only his officers, but his friends, men whose strengths and weaknesses he understood. This one was brave and cautious, that one brave and reckless. This one was quick in thought and action, that one slow to convince and tenacious in battle. This one was a bookstore owner from Boston, that one a farmer from Virginia, this one a New Yorker of independent means, that one trying to support a family in New Hampshire on his army pay. General Washington looked at them and knew them for what they were. They were men who had in common this thing: they were sacrificing themselves for a cause. They had faith in that cause and they were willing to go on fighting and suffering until that cause was won or until it was lost and they themselves were lost.

There they were, waiting: Knox with his fat, round intelligent face; Glover, stubby and stern; the brilliant Greene, perhaps the wisest; Lord Stirling and DeFormay, the professional soldiers; Stark, an unleashed fury; Forrest, the artilleryman; dark-skinned, slim Alexander Hamilton; and young, daring James Monroe. Yes, they were there, waiting.

He spoke calmly, almost as though he were thinking out loud. "Gentlemen, I know that many of you know some of the things that will be discussed here today. I doubt if all of you know everything. It is imperative, now, that we consider again our position and the plans that may lessen its uncertainty." He paused, then started again. "First, as you know, General Charles Lee has been captured at Basking Ridge in New Jersey, a blow that is almost too much."

There was a hum of comment from about the table and Colonel Knox expressed an opinion. "We agree whole-heartedly that General Lee was invaluable as a tactician, but we doubt that his loyalty to you, sir, was all that it should have been."

General Washington's expression did not change and there was no hesitancy in his answer. "The facts, as I see them, do not seem to warrant your statement, Colonel."

The impetuous Captain Hamilton joined Knox's side. "I, too, fully believe, sir, that General Charles Lee's knowledge in battle was invaluable, but day by day my opinion of his full cooperation has lessened."

General Washington's voice took on a shade sterner tone. "Nevertheless, gentlemen, General Lee is not now available and I feel his loss at such times as these."

"His men! Where are his men?" interrupted General Greene. "We know they were not so indiscreet as to get captured."

General Washington sensed the disapproval of his officers on his determined stand for General Lee. "General Sullivan of New Hampshire is in command," he said. "Instructions have been forwarded directing him of the route to pursue in joining us."

"Lee claimed he had four thousand trained troops," stated Greene.

"They should be well-trained," interrupted Lord Stirling. "He's been marching them over half of New Jersey, moving them every which way. It has seemed to some of us that he has been avoiding this camp with the utmost care, and we know his orders directed him here days ago."

"Gentlemen," said General Washington calmly, "instructions and guides have been sent to General Sullivan."

General Greene changed the subject. "And what of General Gates?"

"General Gates is unwell and has gone to Philadelphia."

"It is rumored, to Baltimore, where Congress has fled," said Lieutenant Monroe. "There, I presume, to present his qualifications for the post of Commander-in-Chief. Your present position, sir."

If there was weariness in General Washington, it came into his eyes now. He spoke almost with resignation in his voice. "Gentlemen, these are things of which we are not certain, and they are not the reasons for this council. Will you permit me to proceed with the more urgent things at hand?"

There was a stirring about the table. George Washington waited patiently until the men were silent. Then he spoke. "It is planned that on Christmas Day all the troops will be mustered on the parade ground, and before the muster each of you will read to his men an article I have at hand, written by Thomas Paine, a man you all know and respect. I would like, gentlemen, for you to hear its first few words."

From the table he picked up a pamphlet, waited until every officer was giving full attention, then he read, slowly and clearly: " 'These are the times that try men's souls. The summer soldier and the sunshine patriot will, in this crisis, shrink from the service of their country; but he that stands it now, deserves the love and thanks of man and woman.' "

When he had finished, he placed the paper carefully with the others.

There was no comment from the officers, only silence, a silence that meant approval. General Washington felt the impact of this approval, yet he waited—waited for the exact moment to proceed, and when it came he said, "Gentlemen, it is cold and getting colder; the men are hungry, and they will be hungrier; they are discouraged and they must not become more discouraged. The entire country is discouraged. Not only are men leaving daily for their homes without permission, but daily the citizens are losing faith, and if not actually joining the Tory ranks, at least are doing nothing to further our cause. It grieves us all to accept this fact. Nevertheless, it is a fact. But that fact alone should not be the motive for hasty or unprepared effort on our part. I believe, however, that the time for action is here now, and that we are as prepared as we shall ever be." He paused, then slowly and carefully said, "From recent news and developments brought to my attention, I feel that the time has come to strike—strike before the Delaware freezes and the enemy is at our throats again. If it were possible for us to move our army across the Delaware, I am certain we could surprise this enemy and capture the town of Trenton."

He stopped and the men remained silent. These men, who had hoped for this, were mute at the daring of it.

One man finally stood up, looked confidently about the table, then spoke to General Washington. "Sir," he said, "you may continue with your undertaking. The Fourteenth Massachusetts Continental Regiment, the men of Marblehead, will take you across the Delaware."

There was a sound of approval from the gathered officers, and there was the ghost of a smile on General Washington's lips.

"You will ask the men, John?"

"I will ask them, sir," said Colonel Glover, "whenever you wish."

"Not now, John," said the Commander, hastily. "Not now. Let us first set to the work ahead of us, the planning, and may God guide us."

18

Tom BRIMBLECOM, Acting Corporal of the Guard, Adam Bean, Jethro Hatch, and Matt sat huddled about the midnight fire, guarding the boats anchored behind Malta Island. Tom was speaking. "You should have seen them coming up the main road. Maybe two thousand of them, not any more. Looked like a bunch of walking scarecrows. I don't know what General Charles Lee did to them before he was captured, but right now they ain't good for nothing."

"I thought he had about four thousand first-class fighting men," said Adam.

"First-class fighting men!" said Tom. "Maybe they were once, but they sure ain't now. I thought the Connecticut men were in bad shape, but these men, why, none of 'em had shoes; they were almost naked; and a shoal of 'em had to be helped along by somebody else. I'm telling you those first-class soldiers are going to keep Doc Bond and every other doctor in this army busy for some time to come."

"They'll probably get most of the blankets the Pennsylvanians are gathering," said Jethro. "Seen a wagon load come in just yesterday. The driver yelled to me that there wasn't a spare blanket left between Easton and Philadelphia. Said they had to beg for 'em, fight for 'em, and pay for 'em, but they got 'em."

"That's what we've got to do for everything we get nowadays, isn't it?" said Adam. "Beg for it, fight for it, or pay for it. Matt, be a good soldier and throw a couple of sticks on this fire. I'm about to freeze."

Matt got up stiffly and took a step toward the pile of wood that had been gathered. Suddenly he called to the men, "Look!" He pointed at the sky above the camp. "There's a real fire over there."

The men rose and joined him. "Mackerel!" said Jethro, gazing at the rosy glow on the low clouds. "That must be warming a lot of men."

"That's more than you can say about our fire," commented Adam.

For almost four hours the men had been doing nothing but keeping the fire burning, trying to stay warm, and listening to the moored boats they were guarding as they bumped hollowly against one another when the current and the light breeze disturbed them. Now they watched the sky till the ruddy glow paled, then they returned to their own meager blaze. They were hazarding guesses as to what had burned, when a sound on the path leading down from camp set them on their feet as though they had been jerked up by the same string. Tom Brimblecom stepped quickly into the shadow of the trees, followed by the others. He held his musket at the ready and shouted, "Halt, who goes there?"

From the path a firm voice said, "Friend."

"Advance real slow and stop when I tell you," ordered Tom.

From the darkness came an almost amused voice, "Don't you want the password?"

"There's time for that when I'm looking down my gun barrel at you," shouted the Corporal. "Now, come out slowly into the firelight."

All the men on guard duty leveled muskets at the sound as it came toward them. Then a tall, straight ramrod of a man came into the light thrown by the low blaze, and the blaze flickered on the man's blue and buff uniform and sparkled in the gold of his epaulets.

The guards' guns and jaws dropped at the same time. It was Acting Corporal Tom Brimblecom who recovered first.

"Excuse me, sir, Mr. General," he fumbled.

George Washington let a hint of a smile tip up the corners of his straight, firm mouth. "I think you handled the situation very well, Corporal. What's your name?"

"Private Brimblecom, Acting Corporal of the Guard, sir," answered Tom.

"And the others?"

"Private Bean, Private Hatch, and Private Doliber, sir."

George Washington nodded his head. "Glover's men," he said. "Were you at Pell's Point?"

"Yes, sir," said Tom, Adam, and Jethro, almost together.

"And Long Island," added the General, "and also Cambridge." Then, very low, "John Glover's Fourteenth Massachusetts Continental Regiment." He stared into the fire. "The willing horse gets the load," he said.

"Beg pardon, sir?" said Tom.

General Washington laughed. "I wasn't speaking to

you or the others, Corporal. I was just thinking of what's past and what's ahead. You men always seem to get your share."

Matt stood fidgeting as the General spoke. He hadn't had his share. Hardly knowing that he did it, he blurted out, "I wasn't at those places, sir."

The General turned to him. "No?" he said.

"No, sir," said Matt. "I just came from Marblehead a month ago."

The General smiled. "You're in good company, lad. Can you row a boat?"

"Yes, sir," answered Matt.

"Ain't a man in Marblehead that wasn't born in a dory during a hurricane, sir," stated Tom Brimblecom.

"I'm about certain of that," answered the General. "Corporal, I'm relieving this boy from guard duty. I want him to row me downstream. Can you handle this post without him?"

"Yes, sir," said Tom. "The guard changes in about half an hour."

"There was a small boat put away for me a day or so ago," stated General Washington. "Do you know where it is?"

"I do, sir," said Matt. He knew exactly where the Kinderhook boat was anchored. He had checked it when he had arrived on duty.

"Good night, gentlemen," said the General. "Lad, show me the way."

The men came to attention and saluted briskly.

With General Washington in the stern, Matt eased through the moored boats and into the current. Once they were moving downstream, the General spoke. "I have a task of some importance for you. We are to proceed to a point a mile below the ferry, where you will pick up a man and row him across the river. Now, keep close to the bank; we're not to be discovered by our own patrol boats. When you have delivered your passenger to New Jersey, return and report to me at the Keith House, and mind you this, you are not to speak to anyone till you have done so."

"Yes, sir," said Matt. He tried to keep the awe from his voice. He, Matt Doliber, was rowing General Washington down the Delaware River. He was alone with General Washington, doing a job for him, and an important job, too. Mighty important. He rowed carefully, evenly, smoothly. What would Brad Ferguson think of him now? What would Tink say? He paused in his thoughts when he remembered Tink. Tink hadn't answered roll call that night. What would Paula Kinderhook say? Her turned-up little nose would certainly be pulled down a peg if she could see him now. He'd better stop thinking and pay attention to rowing.

In the dark the General, sitting in the stern, was a slim, erect arrow of a man. Strong, that's what, Matt thought. He leaned forward and caught the water with his oar blades, and slanted back, driving the boat ahead. Strong, even while sitting still. Strength that made you feel it, more strength than Matt's flexing muscles gave, as he pulled long on the oars. A different kind of strength. He wondered why he ever considered leaving an army commanded by such a man as this.

They slid down through the dark cold of the river, silently past McKonkey's ferry building, a black cube against the sky, down along the river's edge, until the tall man in the stern said, "Now let us drift." Matt leaned on the oars.

From the shore came the bawl of a distressed cow—then quietness—and again the sick, bellowing bleat.

"Take me to that sound," said the General. Matt obeyed. It was easier to find the sound than to locate a fog warning on a shut-in night off Misery Island.

"Steady, now," said the General.

Matt touched the land with hardly a jar and held the boat steady. There was no awkwardness about the General as he sprang to the icy shore. Very quietly he turned.

"You've had your orders, lad. Wait here."

He disappeared into the trees, and almost immediately a figure came from them, stepped into the stern of the boat, and said, "Set me down on the Jersey side."

Matt sat almost stunned. He knew that voice, the voice with Ireland in it—John Honeyman's voice. This was a mistake; John Honeyman was a spy; he was to be hanged. Matt sat with his oars poised, unable to move them.

"Pull away, man, pull away," said the voice. "Ye've had yer orders."

19

WHEN THE surprised guard closed the door behind Matt, General Washington rose from the long table and advanced toward the boy. So this was the lad he had met at the campfire and who had followed his instructions. He looked different in the light. He meant to ask him if the orders were successfully completed and to warn him, again, not to speak to anyone, at any time, of the task he had performed; but he hesitated. This couldn't be the same boy—not with those tightly pressed lips and the cold look in his eyes. No, it couldn't be. He knew these fishermen from the New England coast. They were hard, silent men. Years of toil, solitary toil against the sea and wind, had made them trust themselves above all others, and trust no other man until he had been proved. But this wasn't a man, it was a boy.

Then he knew. This boy was not hard and self-sufficient. It wasn't hardness in his eyes. It wasn't coldness in the tight-lipped face. Once he had had a stepdaughter. That was long ago, home in the peaceful stillness of Mount Vernon. She wasn't as bright as this boy; she wasn't so much alive. But he had loved her and protected her; and he could remember her, before she passed away, and sometimes when things went wrong, her eyes and lips took on the look that this boy had. It wasn't a hard look. It was the look of someone who had been hurt. Still he did not speak. He, George Washington, who could give an order that would move an army on the double, was groping for the right words to say to this lad.

He said the only thing he could say. "You got your passenger safely to New Jersey?"

"Yes, sir," answered Matt, flatly.

"You had no trouble?"

"No, sir." Then George Washington knew, for the boy added, "Mr. Honeyman got ashore without anyone seeing him."

The General, with his hands clasped behind his back, walked to the window, gazed into the night, then came back.

"You knew it was John Honeyman?"

"Yes, sir," said Matt. "I was the one who rowed him here, when we captured him."

"Well," said the General, "I hadn't bargained on that."

Now he knew what to say. "Private Doliber, you believe that I, personally, allowed a spy, a dangerous spy, to escape. I did. I alone have taken that full responsibility. There are times in the career of a soldier when it is his duty to obey, and obey blindly, without question, the orders of his commanding officer. Tonight you were selected to perform a duty. Through, shall we say, chance, you were probably the last man who should have been chosen. You have performed part of that duty successfully; however, the hardest part remains"—he paused, then continued—"the part that calls for absolute silence on what has passed tonight. You must tell no one, not now or ever. You must erase it from your mind. I will give you this assurance: what I did was for the good of everyone connected with our enterprise. I suggest that if your fellow guards question you, you convey to them the thought that I was checking the effectiveness of the night-patrol boats." He stopped and almost smiled. "By the way, that might be an excellent idea. I don't remember seeing or hearing one of them." Now the stiffness he had maintained while addressing Matt was gone. He relaxed and held out his hand. "I believe I can depend on your silence and your faith in me."

Matt took the hand, big, bony, and firm. Somehow the doubts that had plagued him were gone. It was all right to take John Honeyman, the spy, to New Jersey. He didn't know why, but it was all right; and he'd never mention it to anyone. He was surprised to hear himself say, "Sir, the boat we used, are we finished with it? I borrowed it from someone and would like to return it."

A small frown wrinkled the General's forehead and disappeared almost as soon as it came. His voice remained relaxed.

"Private," he said, "I'm afraid not. We must keep all the boats we have at the present time, big and little; however, I think that in the future you may recover it. I hope so. Now it will be daylight soon enough. You will oblige me greatly if you will tell the sentry to allow no one else to enter, till dawn at least."

Jethro Hatch was awake when Matt crawled into the

tent and sought his blankets. He raised himself on an elbow and said, "You still a private, Matt? I thought you'd be a colonel by this time. Where you been?"

Matt didn't answer and Jethro continued, "Do you know that fire we saw? Well, it was across the road from the guardhouse and when the guards rushed to put it out, someone broke the lock on the guardhouse door and John Honeyman slipped out slicker than an eel through a cod net. Half the camp is out looking for him now, and the other half, that's us I think, will be out looking for him tomorrow. If I were you, I'd get some sleep."

Sleep didn't come so easily. Matt lay awake wondering what trouble John Honeyman would cause over in New Jersey.

20

J OHN HONEYMAN knew where he was when Matt put him ashore. He would have known where he was at any point on the Delaware all the way down to Camden. He made his way through the darkness of the woods to the road and followed the road to the Abbott farm. Cautiously he crossed the farmyard, slipped into the barn and up into the hayloft, where he went to sleep.

It was a cold, rainy morning when he woke. He hated to crawl from the warm, dry hay that covered him. The guardhouse at camp had offered no such comfort, but he had work to do. He hesitated a minute in the barn doorway, watching the water dripping like a curtain from the eaves, then he hunched his shoulders against the rain and hastened to the road. He was drenched almost before he started. He wished he had something to eat. It would be more than an hour before he met the Hessian outposts. On a day like this they wouldn't be far from their barracks and those that he met would be out of sorts. Guard duty without a fire to lounge about, the water dripping down necks unprotected by peaked, brimless helmets, and the general discomfort of the situation would make the Hessians ill-tempered. He'd have to be carefully alert today.

Head down he plowed doggedly along the soggy road. It was even farther to the first detachment of guards than he expected. They were stationed hardly out of sight of the mist-shrouded buildings of Trenton and were so overcome with their own dismal situation that he saw them long before they saw him. They were big blond bears of men, thick across the shoulder, and pink of cheek. They did not challenge him until he was almost within arm's length. Then their burly sergeant grunted, "Ach, the cow man, und no cow."

The men about him relaxed. "Und not even vun little piglet for the Colonel's Christmas dinner. The Colonel vill be ubset, not even a little piglet. Vare are you going, now?"

"Do ye want a look at me pass?" asked John Honeyman. He put his hand to a soaked pocket.

"No, no," said the Sergeant. "You always haf a pass. Vare you going, now?"

"Sure, and to see Colonel Rall, and who else?"

The Sergeant shrugged. "Mittoudt no cow, mittoudt no small pig. Better you get one first, or you vill not be velcome."

"I'll take me chances," said Honeyman. "It's not Christmas till tomorrow. The Colonel will have his cow or piglet by then. I'll see to that."

"Better off you'd be if you had vun now," said the Sergeant. "I vould stand outside a veek in the rain before I vould face Colonel Rall mittoudt somethings for his Christmas dinner. Now, go avay und don't come back this road, ve don't vish to be bothered."

The room John Honeyman entered was bright with

116

light. A blazing fire flamed on the hearth and a crystal chandelier held a dozen candles, all burning. Colonel Rall sat in a straight chair, his head tilted back, a towel about his neck, and he held a small basin in his hands under his chin. A Hessian, his gaudy blue and red uniform covered with a long apron, was shaving him. A young officer, a lieutenant, sat at a table near the window. He was carefully building a house of playing cards. They said nothing. At last the barber wiped and folded his razor. Then from a bowl of steaming water he took a hot towel, gingerly wrung it and, juggling it from one hand to the other, plopped it onto the Colonel's face. From under it came the sound "Ach!" The card player grinned.

The barber retrieved the towel, shook some of the steam from it, and cautiously draped it about the Colonel's face. With the ends of the towel he removed some small dabs of lather about the Colonel's ears, took the basin from the Colonel's hands, removed the towel with a flourish, and the job was done.

The Colonel straightened up in the chair and patted his pink jowls tenderly, as he poured a flood of guttural German at the barber. The young lieutenant laughed openly, watched his card house tumble, and proceeded to build it over again. The barber, balancing his bowls and basins, started a retreat from the room, thought better of it, put down his equipment and helped the Colonel into his coat. The small attention softened the Colonel's attitude and he watched without malice as the man left.

The Colonel critically checked his appearance in a large mirror hung over the fireplace, then he turned to Honeyman, who stood hat in hand, a pool of water from his sodden clothes forming at his feet. He didn't speak to Honeyman, but to the lieutenant. "You see, Lieutenant Fischer, what did I tell you? He's back."

The words were the first sign that he even knew John Honeyman was in the room.

"You," now he addressed the Irishman, "move over by the fire and dry yourself while you tell me about your visit to the camp of the Americans." Colonel Rall's heavy voice was so cool that it almost hid his interest in his question. "Major Dechau, of the Alt Lossburg Regiment, reports that two days ago his men fired on you crossing the Delaware in an American boat."

"And ye can be sure it wasn't with me own consent that I was a passenger in that boat, sir. Faith, and there I was with me hands bound behind me back with me own cow rope, and not able to move a muscle, as it were."

"And how is it that you are here now?"

"A fire," said Honeyman. "A fine giant of a fire in a barn across from the very guardhouse I was lodged in. Sure, when the guards were taken up with the blaze it was no trouble at all, at all, to scamper away."

Colonel Rall continued to question. "And how did you cross the river?"

Honeyman slapped the side of his soaking trousers and said nothing.

"Ha," said Rall. "You swam. Hear that, Fischer, he swam the river in this weather! Good man, Honeyman!" he exclaimed.

Lieutenant Fischer looked up from his cards. "He's setting a bad example, sir. The first thing you know, Von

Donop will forward orders for all of us to swim the Delaware to attack, instead of waiting for it to freeze over."

"Ha, ha!" roared Rall. Then he grew serious again.

"Just how did they catch you, Butcher?"

"I was looking for a cow," said Honeyman, "and they were on me before I could run."

"Without a fight, you surrendered?"

"Without a fight!" Honeyman pointed to his discolored eye and displayed the broken skin on his knuckles. "There's one lump of a sergeant on the other side who'll never forget that day," he bragged. "But three to one is too many, even for an Irishman."

Rall took a close look at the eye.

"Then they bound me hands behind me back with me own rope and they took me straight to their General. They were great heroes, they were. You'd have thought the three of them had captured yourself."

"Ha," said Rall. "So they took you to their General. General Washington?"

"The very same."

"And they questioned you?"

"For hours at a time, sir. And when I told them nothing, they threw me bodily into a sty of a jail that was like a sieve, and said they'd hang me with the rising of the sun. Faith now, if that barn hadn't taken fire, I'd be dancing on nothing this very minute."

"And they didn't get a word out of you, Butcher?"

"Not a word, sir, not a word. They're shaking in their boots, sir, waiting for the river to freeze from shore to shore. They know they'd never stand up to your trained men."

"Never," said Colonel Rall.

"Ye know yourself how thinly they're spread out up and down the river, sir. And those I saw in camp," Honeyman shook his head in wonder, "I've never seen a poorer lot of humans in me whole life. If they were cattle, I wouldn't take the trouble to slaughter them. They have no food; they have no shoes. Most of them are half-naked, and they're sleeping on the frozen ground, some without even a blanket or a piece of canvas over them. Faith, I was better off than any of them when I was lodged in their leaky jail."

Colonel Rall beamed. "Did you form any idea as to how many there were?"

"That I don't know, but I saw General Lee's men march past. With General—let me see, now. . . ."

"Sullivan," said Colonel Rall.

"That's the man, the very man," said Honeyman. "He was leading them. Maybe a thousand and a few more. Ye know, I've never seen the like. Nakeder and more starved-looking than all the rest tied together. A good half of them ready for the hospital and the remainder hardly able to drag their muskets along behind them."

"Ha," said Rall. He spoke to the lieutenant again. "Fischer, you hear that?"

Fischer answered in German, "Ya, ya."

"Ya," echoed Rall. He turned back to Honeyman. "Butcher, your news is good. Go to the kitchen, get dried, and get something to eat; then go out and find me a fat piglet for Christmas dinner and charge what you will. Fischer, Lieutenant Fischer. Go send the Sergeant for the band. Because of the weather we had no concert while I was being shaved this morning. But we'll have it now, rain or no rain, for I am very pleased. When you have dispatched the Sergeant, return and I will beat you a game of skat before I write my report to Von Donop. Perhaps now, when he hears of this, he will not keep insisting that I waste my time in the building of useless trenches about this town of Trenton."

21

MATT STOOD up and flexed his leg muscles. All morning he had been squatting at the fire with Adam and Jethro, heating lead till it ran like quicksilver and pouring it into molds to form musket balls. Adam and Jethro rose with him.

"That's the last of the lead," Matt said.

"The last till we get another length or two of gutter-spout or some window weights from Philadelphia," said Adam.

"Can't be many spouts or weights left, can there?" asked Jethro. "Seems like every time a wagon comes in from Philadelphia it's creaking with them."

"Lead gutterspouts or not, this is a fine way to spend Christmas," complained Adam. "Generally we get a day off with maybe a little extra to eat and a rifle frolic to watch, with everyone shooting for a first-class prize."

"Maybe there will be something special this afternoon," said Jethro. "Sergeant Cummings said Lieutenant Bray told him there's to be a muster on the parade ground."

"We know that," said Adam, "but it won't be to collect extra rations or to hold a shooting contest."

"You can be certain of that," agreed Jethro. "We'll probably get just a cheery Christmas message saying that instead of one turnip a day for supper, we'll get half a turnip."

"If I wasn't so hungry all the time," commented Adam, "I could easily consider that a cheery Christmas message."

"You'll get a chance to eat now," said Matt. "The men are beginning to gather around the cook fire."

"Help me take the tent down first," said Adam. "There's some blue sky up there, the first I've seen in a couple of days. Maybe the tent floor will dry out before night."

The three of them quickly moved their scanty equipment from the tent, lowered it, and pulled it to one side so that the sun, shining through the clouds at short intervals, could get at the damp ground on which they had been sleeping.

"That ought to dry up the puddles," said Adam. "The sun isn't strong enough to start the frost from the ground, so it won't get any wetter."

The cook shouted, "Come and get your Christmas dinner! It's a-waiting, and it's special. A bit o' beef and a bit o' pork, two kinds of meat, mind you. Boiled squash and boiled turnip, two kinds of vegetables, mind you; a ration of bread, a pint of milk, almost fresh, and, for this occasion, a pinch of salt for everyone."

"Salt!" exclaimed Jethro. "This is a Christmas dinner! Now, where did I put my spoon and pannikin?" He grubbed through the equipment piled near the lowered tent. "The best meal in a month of Sundays, and I got to waste time looking for my eating tools."

The men had scarcely finished their Christmas dinner when down the lane rode Colonel Glover on his big gray horse. Beside him rode his adjutant, William Gibbs. Leaning forward on the pommel of his saddle, the Colonel held a short conference with the officers stationed at the Knowles Creek camp. The drummers were called and the men waited till the drum rolls summoned them. Then they gathered quickly in formation.

"Company 'tention!" ordered the Adjutant. The men snapped smartly to attention. The Colonel said a word to the Adjutant. "Company at ease!" the Adjutant ordered.

The men stood at ease. Colonel Glover dismounted and took his place before them.

"Men!" he bellowed, in his salt-sea voice. "We are to muster on the parade ground shortly, but first . . ."—he undid a button on his greatcoat and pulled out a pamphlet which he held up for all to see—"I am going to read you an article called 'The American Crisis' written by a fellow soldier whom many of you know, Tom Paine. Now listen carefully." Colonel Glover cleared his throat and in a voice that the farthest man in the formation had no trouble hearing, began: "'These are the times that try men's souls. The summer soldier and the sunshine patriot will, in this crisis, shrink from the service of his country; but he that stands it now. . . .'"

The men listened and heard Tom Paine's thoughts on the war, his recalling of past events in the struggle which so many of them remembered, and above all, his hope and confidence in the success of the struggle for freedom. When the Colonel finished, he scanned his silent troops, and he knew that what he had read had a great effect on his men.

For a seaman, and a cobbler, he remounted his horse

quite skillfully. "Adjutant," he called. "March the men to the parade ground."

The drums rolled and the fifes shrieked and they were off.

On the main road they fell in behind the Third Virginians, gliding down from their bivouac area with long, silent moccasined strides. Falling in behind the Marblehead men as they marched down the road was the New Jersey Militia.

The parade ground was almost filled when they arrived. The Massachusetts Artillery, the hardier of the New Hampshire and New York men who had come in with General Sullivan, the New Jersey Continental Line, the Connecticut, Pennsylvania, and Maryland Regiments, were all waiting for the late arrivals. It was a rag-tag army. Save for the Virginians in their buckskins and Glover's men in their leather-buttoned sea jackets, there was nothing in the rags the others wore to distinguish one regiment from another.

When the last squad had been marched in and the parade ground before headquarters was filled, General George Washington came out to stand on the steps of Keith House. The men, hardly waiting for a command, came to attention.

General Washington surveyed the army before him, noting each regiment, each company, and almost each man; if they had been the finest-equipped, smartest-dressed, most expertly trained army in history, he couldn't have been more proud or grateful.

He turned to General Greene and spoke. "The manual of arms, sir."

The order was passed on to the company commanders, and the company commanders in unison with the Adjutant tolled off the commands for musket drill.

"Join your right hand to your musket!"

With one quick motion guns were raised, the butt chest-high. Both elbows were extended.

"Poise your muskets!"

Right hands grasping the muskets shot out holding the guns shoulder high. The left hands slapped down to the men's sides.

"Rest your muskets!"

The left hands grasped the musket below the trigger. The right hands slipped low on the gun stock and the right feet went a step backward.

On the officers went through the manual of arms: sixty commands, in all. And the men carried out the orders as they had never carried them out before. Each command was executed with snap and precision, each movement was performed in unison. When it was done, the men could see the approval in their officers' faces, and they in turn were pleased with themselves.

Now General Washington spoke and his words were relayed to the men by the regimental commanders. "The time we have waited and planned for is at hand. We are going to attack the Hessians at Trenton."

There was a pause and the men forgot they were at attention. It was as if an explosion they were not expecting had occurred in their midst. A sudden wild cheer shook the last of the raindrops from the eaves of the Keith House. It was a full minute before the officers got the excited men back to attention and quiet enough for further information to be given.

When General Washington spoke again he was still solemn with the weight of his task. "Men, as you know, our first problem is to cross the Delaware, a hazardous feat under any conditions, but now doubly so, for the rain of the past few days has created a thaw upstream, and has swollen the river far out of proportion. Now the Delaware is filled from shore to shore with great slabs of ice rushing downstream." He turned from the men and summoned Colonel John Glover.

"Colonel," he said, "I think you understand the risks of the undertaking."

Colonel Glover, stubby and strong, moved to the General's side. "I understand," he said. "Let me speak to my regiment." From the steps his foghorn voice bellowed. "I am speaking to the men of the Fourteenth Massachusetts Regiment. My regiment." He paused for only an instant. "Boys, you've heard General Washington's words. He has told you of the condition of the river. Does any man in my command think the Delaware can be crossed? If he does, let him step forward."

There was no hesitancy. As one man the entire regiment stepped forward.

Colonel Glover turned to General Washington and saluted. "There, sir, is your answer."

General Washington did not show the emotion he felt. "Thank you, Colonel," was all he said. Then he spoke again to the men. "Your officers have their instructions. Thirty rounds of ammunition, three days' rations; each of you will wear a piece of white paper in his hat, and you will gather at McKonkey's Ferry at dusk."

22

As THE FOURTEENTH Massachusetts wheeled away from the parade ground, excitement had taken the place of the monotony of the last weeks. Matt's excitement was tempered by the thought of Brad Ferguson. He wanted to see Brad. He knew one thing: no matter how much the Virginian hated water, he was going to cross the Delaware like anyone else. When the company reached the side road that led to the camp area, he quietly dropped out of line. He was going to intercept Brad as the Third Virginians marched by. He watched them approach and scanned the lines as they passed. Brad Ferguson wasn't with them. As the end of the line drew even with him, he shouted, "Where's Brad Ferguson?"

A long, smooth-striding soldier drawled, "Went down to look at the river. He don't trust water none."

The man marching beside him grinned, looked back, and shouted at Matt, "He sure don't. I'm the one that sat on his head in the boat coming back from Long Island."

Matt fled down the lane to the camp, drew his three days' rations, thirty rounds of ammunition, and a piece of white paper from the supply sergeant. Without a word to anyone he started for the river. Adam Bean saw Matt hurrying up the road and shouted to him. Matt heard him but didn't stop to answer.

One of a group of men at the ferry, busy nailing boards across fence rails, looked up when he approached. The workman spoke. "Ramps for the cannons and horses," he explained. "You Marblehead men are going to be loaded real deep tonight."

"Did you see anyone down here from the Third Virginians?" Matt asked.

The man thought the question over. "A boy about your size?"

Matt nodded. "Maybe a little thinner."

"Didn't wear pants, just a breechclout?" the man continued.

"That's him," Matt answered.

The man chuckled. "He stood just about where you are for a minute looking at the river." He pointed his hammer at the water. "Did you ever see anything like it in all your born days?" He paused, and when Matt didn't answer, said, "Guess that boy never did either. He just stood right where you are and looked at that ice comin' down like runaway horses, didn't say a word for a spell, then he laughed. 'Men,' he said, 'you sure are lookin' at a coward.' Then he turned and left. That's all, just turned and left."

"Which way did he go?" asked Matt. The man pointed his hammer upstream. "Took the road north."

Another worker, who had never stopped nailing, spoke without raising his head. "Ed, if you want to get to Trenton, you'd better keep on hammerin'. Can't you hear that noise up yonder?"

Coming toward them was the sound of cannon already being trundled down to the river bank.

Matt walked up the road that ran beside the Delaware faster than he had ever walked before. Brad was going to the Kinderhook farm. He knew that was where Brad would go. He walked steadily until he was close to the pickets; then he circled about them quietly and came back to the road a distance beyond the point they were guarding. When the river was visible through the trees or when it ran close to the road, he could see why Brad had chosen to run away. The Delaware was high along the banks, almost over it in some places, and thick ice slabs raced down it, swirling and crunching into each other, often tipping end-up to crash down on other slabs and slither off bobbing downstream. It was no summer boat ride to which he planned to bring Brad back.

On he pushed, never slackening his pace, watching ahead at every turn, hoping to get a glimpse of Brad, but he was almost to the farm before he caught sight of him. Brad was taking his time, feeling, thought Matt, that he was safely away from McKonkey's Ferry. Matt was disappointed. He had wanted to overtake Brad before he reached the Kinderhooks, but he was too late. Just around the next bend was the farm. He could slow down a little now. He was warm and out of breath from his exertion. He had to think, too. How could he get Brad away and back to the landing without creating a disturbance or letting the Kinderhooks know why he came? He'd have to work fast if they were to reach the ferry by dusk. He was in sight of the farmyard, still wondering what he would say, when Brad's voice, behind him, stopped him.

He whirled about as the Virginian stepped from behind a roadside tree.

"Hi," said Brad, grinning. "Knew you were trailing me for the last hour. Guess you decided, the same as me, not to take part in the coming battle, is that it? You know, in spite of my high-flown ideas about it takin' a real soldier to pick out the right choice when he has two chances, you can bet, when it comes to water, I'm pickin' the easy one every time. Looks like you've done some pickin' on the easy side, too."

Matt looked Brad over carefully before he spoke. "You're not picking the easy one this time, Brad. I'm picking the hard one for you. I came to take you back to the ferry, and we don't have much time."

Brad stared at Matt and his grin faded. "You came to take me back? I thought you came up here because you didn't want to get into any real fightin'."

"I don't know about real fighting," said Matt, "but I know I'm going to cross the river and you're going with me."

"I ain't goin' back," said Brad. "I ain't crossin' no river like that. I don't have to tell you I'm scared to cross it, even when it's smooth." He pointed to the rushing, ice-packed Delaware. "If you try to take me back to the ferry you'll find it'll be a lot easier to go down to Trenton and bring the Hessians up here. I'm perfectly willin' to wait till the river freezes over and fight on this side."

"You're going to fight on the other side, Brad," said Matt, calmly. "We can start back right now."

"I ain't goin' back," insisted Brad, "and the reason I know I ain't goin' back is you'd have to beat me real good to get me back, and you ain't beatin' me real good, 'cause you can't in the fust place, and you won't in the second place. I saw you sittin' in the corner the last time we were up here and the Seaveys were spoilin' for a fight on the outside. You don't fight nobody, so let's you and me go on up to the house and sit. Then I won't have to cross the river and you won't have to freeze on the Jersey side watchin' a bunch of boats while the real soldiers march off to Trenton to get shot at."

Matt was coldly determined. He didn't shout or move fast. He had traveled at top speed up the Deleware for an hour to do something, and he was going to do it. "Put your rifle down, Brad," he said. "You're going to need both your hands."

He stepped over to the roadside, laid his musket down, squirmed out of his knapsack, and put his powder horn beside them on the ground.

Brad watched him and, with a laugh, did as Matt did. "Too bad for you, Matt," he warned. "I'm quick and I'm fast, either fightin' or wrastlin'. Come on, I'm ready." There was a look on Matt's face that Brad hadn't seen there before. The expression didn't worry him. He had seen it on other faces, in other fights.

Matt advanced determinedly, but it was Brad who made the first attack. He sprang at Matt, his arms flailing. One fist crashed against Matt's upraised arm, the other glanced from his shoulder. And Matt came at Brad.

This was no Tink Cooper, slinking away, Matt thought as he charged. His fists, too, lashed out; one missed the dodging Brad completely, the other grazed Brad's coonskin cap, sending it spinning into the ditch beside the road. Then they met in a bear hug and Matt felt his own hat fly from his head.

Brad's grip was strong, but not as strong as Matt's. Years of pulling on heavy oars had strengthened Matt's arms, back, and chest. He was squeezing the breath out of Brad and Brad felt it. Quickly he thrust a foot behind Matt's and pushed forward. Over they went onto the hard road, and as they landed with a thud, Matt's hold was broken. Brad was up in a flash, breathing hard to fill his lungs. Matt, too, was up, and they met, like two young rams, head on, and down they went again, Matt striving to lock his arms around Brad, and Brad fighting to land a blow that would stop Matt completely. Matt's solid arms smothered every attempt Brad made. Once more over they rolled into the ditch at the roadside. Once more they struggled to their feet only to crash and go down, with the agile Brad again on top. This time Matt heaved upward, like a boat in a heavy sea, and Brad was rolling again in the dirt. Before they could rush back to the attack, a cool voice said, "What a funny place to wrestle."

Matt looked up to see Paula Kinderhook gazing down at him. He looked at Brad sitting in the center of the road. Together they scrambled to their feet.

"My brothers, Mels and Willem, used to wrestle when they were home, but only in the summer, and on the grass where it was soft. Mels won most of the time."

It was Matt who spoke first. "We weren't exactly wrestling," he said. He kept his eyes on the road, not daring to look at the girl again.

The girl turned toward Brad. There was a raw place on his thigh that his breechclout didn't cover.

"You'd better come up to the house and fix that." She pointed to the scraped skin. "Besides," she added, "we've got some Christmas pudding and cakes. I made them all myself."

Brad walked over and picked up his coonskin cap. Then he picked up Matt's three-cornered hat and tossed it to him. "I guess we don't have time," he said. "Me and him," he jerked his head in the direction of Matt, "we got to go down to McKonkey's Ferry right away. We got something to do down there."

23

IT STARTED to rain before Matt and Brad were halfway back to Malta Island. First a few lazy, warning drops fell; then came a driving, slanting downpour that moved them along at top speed and got them to the landing while the boats were still tugging at their mooring lines and the men of the Massachusetts Fourteenth were still waiting. The men, heads deep in the upturned collars of their sea jackets, shoulders hunched against the storm, silently watched the boats and listened to the ice cakes as they crashed out beyond the island.

In the gathering gloom, Matt led Brad through the group of waiting men, peering as he went into faces as he sought out his friends. It was Sergeant Cummings who spied him first.

"Matt, hey, Matt. This way. You just about made it."

Adam grinned. "I told this crew you'd be here," he said.

Matt motioned toward Brad. "We had something to do."

"For a minute we were worried," said Jed Homan. "We're rowing a Durham boat and we've got an open oar. We thought we might have to get Maillet, the teamster, to handle it."

"Humph," snorted Jethro Hatch. "Maillet can't handle anything that won't stop when he says 'Whoa.' Besides, he says he's going to take his horses over to Jersey if he's got to swim across the river with them."

Sergeant Cummings put a hand on Matt's shoulder. "Matt," he said, "I'll feel better handling the tiller with you at one of the oars."

"Can Brad go down the river in our boat?" asked Matt.

"He certainly can if he's got the courage," laughed the Sergeant.

Brad laughed. "Matt's been telling me that he just read a book that says it doesn't take courage. All it takes is discipline."

The Sergeant nodded. "That's Will Breton's book. I let Matt take it the day we got to McKonkey's Ferry. Let me see, that was eleven days ago, wasn't it? A lot has happened since them." He shook his head. "And tomorrow we ought to be in Trenton. Twelve days 'til Trenton. It certainly seems a long time."

Over the howl of the wind and the rain came the command the men had been waiting to hear. Colonel Glover's bull-like voice bellowed. "You've got your orders, men. Now's the time. You know what to do. Boats away!"

24

THERE WAS NO mad rush for the boats. These men had a job to do and knew how to do it. They expertly took their places: Sergeant Cummings standing in the stern, hands on the tiller, the men at the oars. They were too serious about the job ahead of them to laugh at Brad tumbling awkwardly into the bow and getting whacked with the mooring line as it was tossed aboard.

Quickly they eased out from the other boats, and once free, the Sergeant commanded, "One strong pull, men. Now, all together, pull!" The oars cut into the water at the same instant. The boat shot into the current. "We'll run down with the stream!" shouted Cummings.

The boat slid out from behind the island and Cummings fought with the tiller as they reached the ice-packed open river. Then they were squared away racing downstream. There were boats ahead of them and boats following, in a long line. The dark shore slid backward. The ice and the boat raced along together, neither gaining on the other. Brad's knuckles were white as he grasped his rifle. He felt as though he had left his stomach at the landing.

"McKonkey's ahead," barked Cummings. He put his weight against the tiller and the boat veered toward the shore. Adam used his oar to tilt away an ice cake that threatened to crush them. The rain drove down. The bank at McKonkey's was alive with men.

Big, bulky Colonel Knox in charge of the loading shouted, "In here. Pull her in here." The boat touched land with hardly a jar.

"Sergeant, Sergeant!" Colonel Knox boomed through his cupped hands at Cummings. "We're loading you to the gunnels." He turned and gave orders. "Stephen's Brigade! Only the men from Stephen's Brigade. Climb aboard!" Then he gave orders to the boat. "Load her deep, Sergeant. Those that are left, shove into the next boat. There's one pulling in now."

There was a rush from the shore and wet, cold men scrambled aboard. Brad hung onto his place in the bow. The boat sank low in the water. Another boat pulled up alongside.

Sergeant Cummings took over. "Trim the craft, you men. We're listing. Half you men there to the starboard."

The men of Stephen's Brigade looked at him blankly.

"Starboard, men, starboard!" Then the Sergeant realized that these were not men of the sea. "Starboard, to the right side." He pointed. The men moved and the boat was on an even keel. "Give us rowing room, that's all we need. Ready, men? Now, all together, pull!"

Brad had long since been landed on the New Jersey side along with Stephen's Brigade, the first detachment to cross the river and the brigade that circled out in the dark to guard the landing.

Now it was midnight and the driving rain still slanted into the men's faces as they bent to their oars and guided boats loaded to the gunwales, boats that veered downstream in the wild current and shuddered under the jarring crashes of ice cakes that continually drove them from a straight course. Sturdily rowers fought against the river and the men who were not rowing fought desperately to slant away the ice.

The army on the west bank, waiting for each returning boat, grew smaller ever so slowly. Colonel Knox still ordered and directed in a voice that roared above the storm. "Mercer's Sixteenth! Mercer's Sixteenth, climb aboard." And men sloshed about in rain water now ankle deep in the bottoms, and found seats where they huddled, half-frozen by the icy wind that bore the rain down the Delaware. Then the men of Marblehead strained at the oars and the boat edged away toward the flickering light on the far shore, and when they returned there were more men marching down to the landing.

"Forrest's Battery, Forrest's Battery!" Cannon rolled down to the river's edge. "Keep that boat firm against the shore, men. Steady, steady. Now, swing that ramp aboard! Swing!" The men stood knee-deep in the river and swung a fence-rail ramp from the land to the boat's gunwale. Then inch by inch they coaxed a cannon up the ramp. "Easy, men. Easy does it. Now, lend a hand everybody, lend a hand! Take it down and watch it. If it drops it'll go clear through the bottom. Lower away!"

Bare, bull strength lowered the cannon. Men filled their lungs with damp night air.

"Shove that gun forward, there's another waiting. You're taking three this trip."

"Three? What do you think this is, a man-o-war? Two's all this craft will carry!"

Three cannon were loaded and forty rounds of shot and three kegs of powder and half a dozen artillerymen— and they made it across.

General Washington on the Jersey side sat on an overturned beehive and watched every move, counted every minute.

Then there were the wild-eyed horses, blindfolded and urged aboard by iron fists knotted in bridles and by soft words. "Steady, boy, steady." They trembled frantically till firm ground was once again beneath their hoofs and gentle hands stroked the glistening necks till the voyage was forgotten.

Now, more men, and more cannon, and more horses. Yes, they were late, hours late, but the lateness only added to the men's efforts.

One o'clock. Two o'clock. Not rain any more, but sleet and driving snow. Across the river and back, over and over. Three o'clock, and this was the last boat; there was no one left on the west bank. They were all across; not a cannon was missing, not a horse left behind, not a man lost.

"The Third Virginians—where's the Third Virginians?"

"They ain't here, you lummox, this is the Eighth Connecticut. Can't you tell we got pants on?"

"Stirling? Lord Stirling?"

"He's up ahead with his men."

"Glover's regiment, the Fourteenth, fall in here. Come a-movin', a little rowing never hurt anybody. Kept you warm when everybody else froze."

"Come on, come on. 'Now is the time to try men's souls,' you summer soldiers! Fall in, fall in. Mercer, Greene, Hamilton, Monroe, DeFormay, Stark!"

"Sullivan on the left, close your ranks!"

"Knox, Colonel Knox! Artillery to the front!"

"So your powder's wet, what do you think your bayonet's for?"

"A little snow never hurt anybody. What do you want a fire for? Want to roast to death? Fall in, fall in! We're ready, we're ready. Men, we're ready. Forward! March!"

And they marched—without music, without rhythm, without cadence; but it was a march. Down through a wooded aisle to the road, and on, and on, a rod, a mile, a rod, two miles, they went. Step by step, they marched, with clothing plastered to wet bodies, clothing tattered too badly to shield against the driving wind. Cold aching bodies carried by cold aching feet. Cut feet, feet too numb to feel pain, leaving behind a trail of blood where they trod. On and on, they marched, silent, hungry, weary, their unprotected shoulders bruised by the weight of icy rifles held firmly in white-knuckled, raw, wet fists, and the brave piece of white paper each wore in his hat was a soggy badge of honor. Now half of them swerved away to the inland road, and the other half didn't know they had gone. They would meet again, and it was late, late, late. The rain was gone and the road was freezing and tired feet slithered. A man was down, then another and another, but only for an instant. Up and on again. And the sky grew gray. Six miles, seven miles, eight miles. A dog barked and a cock crowed against the leaden skies, and the half that had taken the inland road was met and on they marched. Then suddenly the wind that whistled in the trees carried to those who brought up the rear the sound of crackling rifle fire. And it was daylight, and there was Trenton.

25

To MATT, standing nervously in front of the bridge that crossed Assunpink Creek, the battle for Trenton was an unreal scene flashing in wet color before him. The movement, the acrid smell of burnt powder confused him. It was Adam Bean and Sergeant Cummings, close by his side, who brought the battle into reality for him. "This is one end of Queen Street," explained the Sergeant. "A half a mile straight ahead is General Washington attacking from the other end. That's his artillery firing now, with Greene's, Stirling's, and DeFormay's regiments, he's blocked off that end of the town. On the left is St. Clair and his Pennsylvanians with Mercer's New Jersey Militia. On the right is Assunpink Creek, which is too deep to cross. The enemy's only outlet is to storm this bridge. We'll be in for it soon enough."

Sergeant Cummings was right. Down Queen Street came a scarlet-clad regiment.

"The Alt Lossburgers. We should get it now," shouted Adam. Matt was held spellbound at the sight. If he had wanted to run, he felt that his legs would never carry him.

On came the Hessians, drums beating, battle flags flying, cannon rolling.

General Sullivan's command rang out: "Massachusetts, New Hampshire, and New York men, hold fast!"

Why doesn't someone do something, thought Matt, before they are on us?

Someone did do something. From the left came St. Clair and his Pennsylvania Riflemen. Quietly determined, they trotted across the fields and up the lanes leading to Queen Street. Their first volley struck the Hessians the length of their flank. It was as if a wind had struck them. They swayed as their frantic officers tried to hold them on the road. The second Pennsylvania volley struck them and they broke and fled, not back the way they had come, but to the right along the creek, searching for a crossing. The road was dotted with prone scarlet uniforms. A horse, on which a brilliantly clad officer once rode, raced back toward the town, its dangling reins doing a wild dance as it fled. Along the creek the Alt Lossburgers blundered into a swamp that trapped them and mired their cannon hub-deep in half-frozen muck. Here they tried to rally while the cannoneers fought to free the guns. The relentless Pennsylvanians followed. Hopelessly the Hessians abandoned their cannon, fought their way to higher ground, and rushed, without order or courage, back into town to join Rall, the commander, and his men, milling about in the streets.

The Pennsylvanians trotted back to Queen Street and held their position.

"Well," said Sergeant Cummings, "they did what they were supposed to do."

"Never saw it done better," said Adam.

Matt could breathe again.

144

Suddenly the windows in Queen Street spouted fire, and the confused Hessians swarmed away from the streets and into an orchard near the creek.

"Mercer's men are in the town," shouted the Sergeant. "And here comes Knyphausen's Regiment. They want those cannon in the swamp." From the orchard came the black-uniformed Knyphausen Regiment. They skirted the edge of the swamp and formed solidly about it, while frantic artillerymen tried to free the sunken Alt Lossburger guns. The men holding the bridge stood firm and the Pennsylvania Riflemen advanced again, trotting steadily, doggedly, at the black-clad regiment; and the proud Knyphausen Regiment broke as the Alt Lossburgers had before them. They ran, not back to Rall in the orchard, but up along the stream, looking for a place to cross. They advanced too far, and Greene and Stephens pinned them in the bend of Assunpink Creek and held them there.

A quarter of a mile away, in the orchard, Colonel Rall was attempting to get order out of confusion. Bewildered, the enemy moved back toward the town. "They're going to try to retake the buildings!" shouted Sergeant Cummings. "Look!"

From the top of Queen Street moved the Third Virginians. Not deadly, quietly, efficiently, like the Pennsylvania Riflemen, but they came wildly screaming like a hurricane that swept everything before it. The Hessians fled back into the fields.

"They must come this way now," said Sergeant Cummings. "We've got to meet them."

Matt never heard the order that sent them forward. All he knew was that he was rushing with Marblehead, New

145

York, and New Hampshire men, past the Pennsylvanians, who fell behind them to guard the bridge, past the still red and black figures lying in the mud, then across the fields and up a gentle slope where on the crest the men dropped to the ground and poured a withering volley into the Hessian ranks. Again he knew the sound of musket balls as they whined above his head. What was it Brad had said? You could always fire back if you didn't get hit and your powder was dry. He fired, reloaded, and fired again.

The blue-coated Grenadiers of Colonel Rall surged toward them, wavered, and stopped. Above the sounds of battle came Rall's heavy German voice as he stood high in his stirrups pointing the line of battle with his sword, urging his men on. "Forward! forward! my Grenadiers!" he shouted.

"A real brave man," said Adam Bean. He sighted his musket carefully and fired.

Colonel Rall's sword dropped from his upraised hand. He swayed in his stirrups and crumpled, sliding into the arms of his men. His Grenadiers did not go forward. It was the ragged Continentals who went forward, and Matt with them, pouring down the slope at the enemy. As he ran he thought he saw the proud Hessian battle flags go down. This was the last thing he remembered. Something that felt like a hot iron seared his leg above the knee. The next step he took felt as if he were stepping on nothing. He landed jarringly on the hard ground, his musket flying from his hand. Then he rolled over and lay still.

26

MATT DREAMED he was in a small boat on a choppy sea, lurching this way and that, and he was lurching when he awoke. It took him a while to realize that he was in a baggage wagon. Above him the loose canvas covering shook and trembled with every wheel turn in the frozen road. He winced and quickly reached for his thigh. It was thick with wrappings. He remembered he had been with Sergeant Cummings and the men, and he had got up from the ground to advance on the Hessians. He remembered, too, that he had started to run and that suddenly his leg had felt as if it were not there when he stepped on it. He hastily felt his leg again to assure himself that it was there. He had been wounded. He took a deep breath and winced again. Ahead and behind he heard the rumble of other wagons. He heard a groan and turned his head. Opposite him lay a boy just a little older than he—a boy with overpink cheeks and thick yellow hair. Showing from the edge of the blanket that covered him was a blue and gold collar. A shoulder, half seen, bore the markings of a Hessian lieutenant. The boy's wide blue eyes looked into Matt's. Neither spoke for a long while. The boy groaned again as the wagon swerved in a rough stretch of road. He breathed quite hard all the time. The canvas over their heads trembled constantly.

The boy spoke first, but not to Matt. He was mumbling to himself, and Matt did not understand him. He turned and looked into the boy's face, and with an effort the boy said, *"Mein Oberst Rall, mit him alles ober."* Then, noting the puzzled look on Matt's face, he spoke in halting but precise English. "My Colonel Rall, with him all is over."

Matt knew what the boy meant. The commander of Trenton was dead. Matt wanted to say something, but he couldn't think of anything to say. A long while passed before the young Lieutenant spoke again.

"The butcher," he said in English, "the butcher, Honeyman, the butcher. I was there with my Colonel, when he. . . ." The boy stopped and coughed, and when he had finished coughing, took a deep, rattling breath. "When he," the boy continued, "when he said there could be no battle. The Americans were too ill-equipped to fight. I heard him say that. Was it yesterday, or the day before? I don't know, I can't remember." His voice trailed away to nothing.

Matt lay still, thinking. John Honeyman had told Rall there could be no battle? It was a question he found hard to answer. How could it be? Why would John Honeyman tell the Hessian commander that there would be no battle? It came to him suddenly. The tall, thin Irishman was not a Tory. Honeyman was an American, a very clever American, risking his life every day for his country, entering unafraid the enemy camp, into the very presence of the commanding officer, and keeping him off his guard and unprepared for battle. No wonder General Washington had aided the man in escaping. No wonder the General had sworn him to secrecy. No one must ever know about John Honeyman.

The cart jogged on from rut to rut. Matt listened to the sounds of the other carts. His leg throbbed. The Hessian across from him spoke in German for a while and then was quiet.

German, thought Matt. German was the writing on the mug Paula Kinderhook had given him. He looked at the boy, and when the boy looked back he said slowly, "What does '*Wenn Sie einsam sind, ist unser Haus Ihres*' mean?"

If the boy was surprised at the odd question, he did not show it. He stared at Matt for a long while. Then slowly he wet his lips. "You do not pronounce my German very well," he said.

"Do you know what it means?" Matt asked again.

"Yes," said the boy, "I know what it means." He paused to take a deep, painful breath. "It means"—his words came hard—"it means 'When you are lonely, you can call this house your home.' " He smiled a weak little smile, and his eyes turned upward to look at the trembling canvas.

Matt heard the teamster shout to his horses, and the team shuddered to a stop. Then there were sounds that he knew: the sound of rushing water, the hollow thud of boats moored close together, and, a little ways off, the squeal of oars in dry oarlocks. McKonkey's, he thought. Back at McKonkey's. The horrible jouncing that seemed to be tearing his leg apart would be over for a while. My,

but he was tired. He looked across at the young Lieutenant. The boy's face was no longer pink, but almost color-
less. He was mumbling faintly again in his own language. As Matt watched, his wide eyes opened with an
almost amazed look. They found Matt's and he spoke
softly, ever so softly. "I, too, am lonely, but I'm going
home." He shut his eyes and a tear slipped out from his
long, light lashes and ran down his white cheek.

There were voices outside the wagon and the sound of
feet on the hard ground. The canvas covering parted in
front and the driver peered into the wagon. It was Maillet, the company teamster. Maillet's head disappeared.
The canvas opening closed and Maillet shouted, "There's
two of them in here, sir. Matt Doliber, he looks all right,
but the Hessian is dead."

27

MATT SAT deep in a chair, his wounded leg stretched straight out on a stool before him. He was warm in the sunlight that flooded through the window. There was a rude crutch on the floor beside him. For almost a week he had made short trips about the room with it.

"You won't need that very long," said Doctor Bond, when he had given it to him. "A month or two maybe. By then you'll be as good as new. You'll have a limp for a long time to come, though. Not much of a limp; a person will hardly notice it. But there'll be no more soldiering for you."

"Can I row again?" asked Matt.

"Row!" snorted the doctor. "Sure you'll be able to row."

"Then I'll be able to work with Uncle Eb," Matt said, simply. "I guess I'll go back there, when I can make it."

To Matt the room seemed especially empty. Not so long ago it had been filled with men, men stretched on the few cots available, the rest lying side by side on the floor and overflowing out into the hallway, men tortured with wounds and illness. There had been visitors, too: Sergeant Cummings, Adam, Jethro in a fine new pair of boots,

Tom Brimblecom, and Jed Homan; even Maillet, the teamster, had come in. Some came to stand awkwardly beside him, stumbling over the few words they wanted to say. Others, like Sergeant Cummings, came to sit and speak of the Battle of Trenton, the new victory at Princeton, the Continental Congress, and how it had granted General Washington money and power to continue with the war.

"Matt," the Sergeant had said, "Trenton has changed the whole course of freedom."

Once General Washington and his aides came through, stopping before each man to say a word. At Matt's cot Colonel Glover spoke. "General, this is Matt Doliber, one of my boys."

George Washington looked down at Matt and smiled gently. "Colonel, he is one of my boys, too."

Now Matt was sitting warm in the sun, and alone, the only patient left in the building. Doctor Bond had been in only an hour ago.

"Matt," he spoke with concern, "I don't believe I know what to do with you. You're not bad enough off now to be carried all the way to the hospital in Bethlehem, and you're not well enough to start out on your own for Marblehead. It will be a month or so before you can do that. We've got to decide something pretty soon, because the Fourteenth has gone and I've got orders to join them. I've got to figure out something and while I'm doing it, don't sit in that chair all day. Get up and move about a little, get the blood flowing in that leg. It's going to need plenty of exercise before you can throw that crutch away."

When the doctor had left, Matt had hobbled around

the room a time or two, but it was so pleasant just sitting that he hadn't tried it again.

Outside the window, where such a short time ago the activity of an army filled the area, the scene was desolate. Inside only the occasional footsteps of an orderly gathering together the last of the hospital equipment were heard.

Half the morning had gone when Doctor Bond returned. "Matt," he announced, "I've some news for you, and for me, too, I hope. There's a half-naked Virginian outside who says he's come to take care of you. Do you know any Virginians?"

Matt sat up straight. "Yes, I do." He started to rise and the doctor let him rise alone. Holding to the back of the chair, Matt tucked the crutch under his arm.

"Wait, wait," warned Doctor Bond. "Take it easy, now, don't get excited. How can that half-savage take care of you?"

"I don't know," said Matt, "but if he says he can, he can."

Suddenly Brad was standing in the doorway. He held out a pair of fringed moccasins. "I made them from the hide of the deer we got," he said.

Matt reached for them. "They're real soft, aren't they?"

"Sure they're soft," said Brad.

Matt grinned. "And you don't know how anyone could walk in hard boots."

They both laughed.

"Well, young man," said Doctor Bond, "didn't you say you were going to take care of Matt, here?"

"I sure did," agreed Brad. "I ain't got all week to do it

153

either. We'd better get goin'. Fact is, I only got till sundown. Been marching all over Pennsylvania showin' off the Hessian prisoners. Came back last night, and we're leavin' right soon to spend the rest of the winter in the Morristown hills."

"But I can't go to Morristown," protested Matt.

"Who's takin' you to Morristown? Doctor," Brad turned to Doctor Bond, "there's some people we know up river, they say Matt can stay with them till he gets solid enough to go home. They'll treat him fust rate."

"The Kinderhooks?" asked Matt.

"Sure, the Kinderhooks," answered Brad. "I just came from there. Old Kinderhook and the girl, if you can stand her, will take care of you."

Matt tried to keep his voice as calm as possible. "I guess old Kinderhook is all right," he said.

"Boy," said Brad, "you better think up some new things to tell him about them 'Mobblehedters' he's always askin' about. Say, come to think of it, you can add what you Mobblehedters did at the Battle of Trenton. Folks'll be talking about that for a long time to come." He paused, then with a sly look he said, "Of course, if you don't want to go where that girl is. . . ."

Matt interrupted hastily, "If Doctor Bond says so, I guess I'd better go." He tried to keep the eagerness he felt from showing through the words.

Inside he was feeling awfully good.

The doctor spoke to Brad. "You're taking a load off my mind, young man, if you have friends up the river who will take care of Matt. He can certainly go; that is, if it isn't too far. Matt's not able to travel any distance with that crutch and I've got nothing available that would get him there."

"He can go as far as the ferry, can't he?" asked Brad. "It's not a quarter of a mile from here."

"We can get him to the ferry, all right," answered the doctor.

"The rest will be easy," said Brad. "I've got a boat that belongs to the Kinderhooks, and Matt is going to take it back."

Matt stared at Brad in amazement. "Me! I can't row yet, Brad."

"Of course he can't row!" said Doctor Bond.

"Who said anything about him rowin'? I'm rowin'!" Brad laughed. "Guess you never heard of me. Nowadays, out back of Winchester, Virginia, they call me 'Fresh-water Ferguson.'" He walked over and put an arm around Matt's shoulder. "You're takin' the boat back. You'll be in full command. I'm the kind of a crew that needs a fust-class captain. Now," his voice was again loud, "you'd better get packed and down to the river right quick. If I ain't mistaken, I'd say that girl with the yellow braids is waitin' on the river bank by the farm this very minute."

About the Author

John Duncan was born in Gardner, Massachusetts, but he spent most of his early years in Corning, New York, and in Philadelphia. He attended the University of Oklahoma and received a B.F.A. in Education. He is now in the Office of the Division of Employment Security, Portsmouth, New Hampshire, and he and his wife, the former Lillian Perkins, live in nearby Madbury, New Hampshire. Mrs. Duncan is a librarian at the Durham, New Hampshire, Library.

TWELVE DAYS 'TIL TRENTON is John Duncan's second book of historical adventure for young people. His earlier DOWN THE MAST ROAD is the exciting story of a boy who joins a crew going into the woods to bring out a mast pine for a new ship.